1

HARRISON HAWK

Sequoia Mountain Man

HARRISON HAWK

SEQUOIA MOUNTAIN MAN

(a book of Adventures in the Wild)

by

Connor Corkill

TABLE OF CONTENTS

EPISODE 10 – Franklin -Sawtooth Loop - Hitchhiking – Franklin Lakes – Bear Attack – Forester Lake – Soda Creek – Columbine Lake – Monarch Lake

EPISODE 11 – Survival Mode - Vermillion Resort – The Ferry – Cliff Meadow – The Raven – Silver Pass Lake – The Mountain Lion – The Long Way Home

EPISODE 12 – The Volcano - Farewell Gap Trail – Franklin Pall – Kern River Ranger Station – The Volcano – Coyote Pass – Buillion Flats – Big Blackie

EPISODE 13 – High Sierra Trail - Crescent Meadow – Bearpaw Meadow – Hamilton Lake – Kaweah Gap – Big Arroyo – The Ghost – Moraine Lake – Kern River – Crabtree Meadow – The Cowboy - Mt. Whitney

EPISODE 14 – The John Muir Trail – Yosemite Valley – Tuolumne Meadows – Kyra – Devil's Postpile – Silver Pass Lake – Edison Lake – Thunder & Lightning – Snow-Covered Trail – Rae Lakes – Mt. Whitney – The End

ACKNOWLEDGEMENTS

Ronald C. Gonzales, the author's brother,

who was the character, "Pablo"

My name is Harrison Hawk. I have had numerous adventure stories in mountains, primarily in the Sequoia and Kings Canyon National Parks. Most were amazingly wonderful experiences in picturesque scenes of the high country, with diverse vegetation, and wildlife but there were many other adventures where I was fighting for my life against Mother Nature and all of its mighty power.

I was born in Visalia, California in 1940 to my mother, Eleanor Harrison, an English woman from London, England and my father, Benjamin Hawk, a descendent from the Native American Indian tribe of Yokuts, of the San Joaquin Valley. They lived in the foothills and the valley floor but walked the mountains of the Sierra Nevada.

My grandfather, Elijah Hawk, was an activist hoping to establish laws to help his race of people have more rights but had a hard time because of extreme prejudice among the white Americans who were in power in the government sector. My father and grandfather, Benjamin, moved to London to work with my mother's family who breeds race horses. They, Benjamin and Elijah, changed their first names into biblical or Anglo names in order not to cause any potential problems of racial or religious prejudice among Europeans. Because of that, they named me Harrison Hawk at birth, using the surnames of my mother and father

When I turned 20, I attended a junior college in the Valley and learned about the history and biology of the Sierra Nevada Mountains, taking courses like Wildlife Biology, Forestry,

Firefighting, and History of the great Sierra Nevada mountains. In two years, I graduated with an Associate degree and decided I wanted to walk the mountains that my ancestors walked, to see the beauty that they saw, to experience whatever Mother Nature offers me, whether good or bad.

My great grandfather, Little Red Hawk, lived in Three Rivers, a foothill town at the base of Sequoia National Park. After buying a backpack, sleeping bag, and all essentials for backpacking, I went to see him. He lived in a small three-room adobe house on the outskirts of the city limits. When I knocked on the door there was no answer, so I walked to the back yard and there he was working on his garden with a hoe.

"Do you remember me, sir? I asked.

He looked at me, then walked towards me and studied my face.

"You are Ben's son, aren't you? You have his eyes and you are built big like him."

"Yes, sir, I'm Harrison Hawk."

"Well, son, what are you doing here in Three Rivers?" he asked

"I just graduated from college, sir, and I want to explore the mountains and see what our forefathers saw and experienced."

"Call me "Papo", like you used to when you were a boy." he said.

"Well, my son, I have many stories about when I roamed the mountains as a young man." he said, as he put his hand on my shoulder.

He told me about the dangers he experienced with Mother Nature, including fighting with a bear, and getting lost in a snow storm.

He looked at me with a squint in his eye and said....

"But I would gladly go back, if I could. I love the mountains and the risk is worth taking because the beauty of the high country is majestic and magnificent with its peaks of granite and lakes that are so clear, you can see the trout swimming near the bottom". He closed his eyes, looked upward and smiled as his mind recalled his experience.

"That's what I want to see, sir. I want to go there for weeks at a time, to follow the trails and hike cross-country to remote places where our ancestors walked." I interrupted excitedly.

"In this day and age, men have already conquered those places......but they never change. It would be a great learning experience for you, my son." he said.

"I bought a Kelty backpack and it is completely full with all provisions I need for two weeks." I said.

I showed him my pack and told him everything I had in it.

"Yes, you learned well in that college. You are now ready for a great adventure. Where are you going first?".

"For my first solo backpack trip, I decided to start at Southfork Campground, here in Sequoia National Park, and hit the Garfield Grove Trail, where there's a stand of Giant Sequoias. The trail is 12 miles long and it will take me to Hockett Meadow. Once I get there, I will make a base camp and then take day hikes to Evelyn Lake and Cahoon Rock. I want to see the grove of giants and camp there."

"That is a tough trail....over 5,000 ft. of elevation gain, eleven miles, and it's on a north face, where the sun won't shine much at all so it will have some snow on parts of it in this early June month.", the old man said as he cautioned the novice.

I pulled out a map from my pack.

"There used to be a trail made by our ancestors that went from Cahoon Rock, down the mountain, close to Homers Nose and back to Southfork Campground. I'd like to try that on the way back." I said.

"Yes, I heard of it but it will be hard to follow…..it is not maintained by the Park Service and they discourage anyone to hike on it." he said.

My great grandfather called a friend to take me to the trailhead. He then put his hands on my shoulders and looked into my eyes. "Whenever you feel that you may be in danger…..don't panic. Pray to the Great Spirit and He will help you. He has never failed me and He won't fail you if you are sincere in your prayers." Those were the last words he said to me before I left.

Nick, the driver that was to take me to the trailhead, was also part Yokut Indian. He had a big smile on his face all the time and told me he loved horses. He said he had been on the Garfield Grove Trail with his horse and had seen a mountain lion in that area.

"Don't worry about that lion." he said. "They usually stalk small game. If you were a child or very short person, then that lion would stalk you and wait for you to start running, then he will attack".

"I can handle myself, Nick……I'm not afraid of the wildlife here. I would be afraid if there were still Grizzly bears here but they are not here anymore."

"You'll be fine, you'll be fine" he said.

We drove past a small bridge and turned right. After two miles, we came to a STOP sign. Straight ahead was the Three Rivers cemetery. We turned right for ten miles and reached the end of the line, the southernmost part of Sequoia National Park. So here, at Southfork Campground was the trailhead of my first solo adventure in the Sierra Nevada mountains.

GARFIELD GROVE TRAIL

We arrived at the trailhead at 10am. I thanked the driver and walked to the trailhead. There was a small area for car parking, which was near a livestock trough inside a small corral. There was a pickup truck with a horse trailer parked there. I figured there would be riders on my trail because horses are not allowed on the Lady Bug Trail, which is a short 1.7 mile trail on the South side of the river after crossing the wooden bridge.

The elevation at the trailhead was about 3,000 ft. and Hockett Meadow was about 8,500 ft. so I knew I had some climbing to do. The trail was well-marked with lots of deer brush, manzanita, and other plants that I had studied in college. As I started the hike, I noticed the sun was shining on my trail but I knew it wouldn't last long. It will get shady and cold soon. I also noticed there were horseshoe marks of the trail and that explains the horse trailer that I saw in the parking lot by the trailhead. I noticed large batches of poison oak by the trail. "Leaves of Three, Let them Be" came to mind.

After I hiked about one mile, I saw a spur on the trail that went left, downward toward the river. It was not a clear, maintained trail and I remember Papo telling me that there was a grassy trail that leads to Soldier Cave, which had steel bars at the entrance. It was put there by the Park Service to prevent vandals from entering and defacing the walls and destroying the stalactites and stalagmites growing inside the cave. I went to the foot of the entrance but turned around and continued onto the main trail, since I had a long way to go, before I can make camp for the night somewhere.

Four miles from the trailhead, I heard a growl. I stopped….slowly turning my head around and looked behind me……I saw nothing. It sounded like a mountain lion and I immediately thought about Nick and what he said about it. I knew that mountain lions will stalk someone if they are alone and if I would try to run, he would drag me down. I couldn't run anyway since I had a 50-lb. pack on my back. My heart started beating faster anticipating the lion coming after me. I stood still for about a minute, then started to walk again slowly…..then another growl….I stopped. I decided to let the cat know that I wasn't afraid of him, even though I was. I yelled as loud as I could, scolding him for being a bad lion. I waved my arms as if I was daring him to attack me. All that time, my heart was pounding in my chest. I looked upslope and saw his face. I yelled again and he turned and disappeared. I was so relieved. I waited until I got my breath back to a slow, steady rhythm, then continued on.

The trail started changing from a chaparral type of vegetation into a pine forest. I looked down towards the Southfork River and saw one Giant Sequoia but it was an isolated tree away from the grove. A tiny seed must have blown away from the grove over 1,000 years ago, planted itself in isolation and persevered. The oak trees and manzanita were getting more and more scarce the higher I climbed. It was now white fir trees and ponderosas mixed into that transition zone of woodlands and pines.

As I continued on, I saw a rope on the side of the trail. It looked thick and of a grey color. I picked it up and realized it was a rope bridle for a horse. It must belong to the horse party that I assumed was ahead of me. I was hoping they were not coming down on the trail as I'm going up because I would have to climb upslope to let the horses through. Horses and mules pretty much have the right of way on mountain trails. I took my backpack off and secured the bridle with a carabiner that I had hanging on the side of my pack. I thought the horsemen would probably thank me for finding the bridle and returning it.

After climbing 5 miles, my 50 lb. backpack felt like it weighted 100. I was really getting tired. I looked to my left and across the Southfork River. I saw the sun shining on the Chaparral vegetation across the river....thick sagebrush and manzanita whereas on my side of the river, the North side, I was in the shade, there were snow patches, and it was colder. I knew there would be some pain on and off the trails but I wanted to experience what my ancestors experienced.

GARFIELD GROVE

I finally reached the beginning of the Garfield Grove in the afternoon. There in front of me was one huge tree that had a diameter of 80 or 90 inches. It reminded me of my Timber

Cruising days for the Forest Service during the Summer months of my college years. As I kept walking towards the grove, I saw a snow field on my upslope just ahead. As I got closer, I realized it was a small canyon-like depression with snow covering the top of it, a snow bridge. The floor of the mini-canyon was dry and the strong breeze blowing under the snow bridge was bitterly cold. I looked at my map and realized it was Snowslide Canyon. I walked another 50 or 60 yards and to my left there were about 7 or 8 Giant Sequoias and, to my relief, there was one campsite right under one of the giants. It even had a grill over the fire pit. I was happy to rest a bit but, since there was a full canopy of tree limbs over me, the sunless environment was very cold. I took off my backpack and leaned it against the giant. My canteen was almost empty. I had to find water before dark, I thought. I looked at my watch and noticed that I had two hours before twilight time. I opened my backpack, took out a granola bar, ate it and downed it with the last of my water. I took out my North Face tent and brown ground tarp. I spread out my tarp on the moist but level area of the campsite and pitched my tent. I hurried up and threw my sleeping bag and pad into the tent. As I looked in my pack, I removed my food, which was in a duffel bag.

I looked around for a tree branch to hang my food. If I didn't, a hungry bear might just visit me during the night and steal it. I found an oak tree with a good straight branch that was about twenty-five feet high and stretched out about ten feet horizontally. I unwrapped my fifty-foot nylon rope from my pack, looked for and found a flat granite rock, half the size of my hand. I tied the rope around it, took aim and hurled the rock over the branch. I finally got it over where I wanted it, making sure it was far away from the trunk of the tree so a bear cub couldn't reach it. Mother bears have been known to teach their cubs to climb trees and snatch hanging food from careless backpackers. The weight of the rock came down slowly. I untied the rock and replaced it with one of my carabiners. I walked to my backpack with food in hand. I made sure I would always keep my food with me at all times or a bear could appear suddenly and take it. I opened my pack and took out another duffel bag with my toiletries, i.e., toothpaste, soap, etc.. After equalizing both bags by weight, I connected one to a 'biner, made a large loop with the slack and hoisted one bag upward about fifteen feet with my six-foot staff, which has two golden brass hooks back to back at the end. I then connected the other bag to another 'biner and raised the second bag so both bags are hanging evenly from the ground.

 After hanging my food, I looked at my watch......one hour till dark. I took out another duffle bag containing my dry clothes, took out a black flannel shirt and put the rest in the tent. I took off my sweaty T-shirt and quickly put on a dry one. Now I had to find water. I grabbed my two canteens and walked up the trail about 50 yards where I found a small trickle of water flowing down a brook. I bent down, found some rocks to build a small dam so I could fill my canteens. After walking back to camp, I decided not to cook, since it will be pitch dark very soon. I chewed on some beef jerky and drank water. I took my boots off and put them in the tents vestibule. When I got a whiff of my dirty, sweaty socks, I just about passed out. I took off my shorts and put on a clean pair of kaki pants and slipped into my sleeping bag.

I thought about what Papo told me before I left...."be sincere in your prayers." I prayed that night that everything would turn out OK. I felt that God was with me and He would lead the way in my journey. I could hear the wind blowing through the trees. There is no sound more beautiful than the sounds of Mother Nature......a natural symphony, as the pitches rise and fall with the speed of the wind through the trees.

I woke up at daybreak, peeked out from my tent and there was a misty fog surrounding my campsite. It was cold and I didn't want to go out just yet. I lay there...warm in my sleeping bag. I thought about finding some dry wood to make a fire. After lying there for twenty minutes, I put on my boots, jacket, and knit cap and looked for firewood. Everything was wet from the fog and high humidity so I forgot about starting a fire. I took my staff and pulled down my food that was hanging on the branch. I took down both duffel bags, since I wanted to move on and not stay another night in this cold, dark grove. I took out my stove and fuel, poured a cup of water in my small saucepan and fired it up. The hot coffee smelled good and made me warmer. After one cup, I heated up another cup and added some dry oatmeal to it. I will need more energy to reach Hockett Meadow. I added a chocolate bar to complete my breakfast.

After eating, I broke camp, dismantled my tent and folded it. I then heard a loud shriek...I looked up and saw a raven fly overhead. I stared at it and a chill went up my spine because my grandfather, Eijah Hawk, told me long ago that the Yokut Indians, my ancestors, believe that when a raven flies over you in the morning, it will bring bad luck. Even though I am not superstitious, it made me wonder if there was any truth to it.

I quickly packed up and hit the trail. I hiked through more small canyons and crossed more streams. When I finally got to Southfork Crossing, I saw that the river was high and moving pretty fast. I took my pack off and I was so exhausted. Since it was already late in the afternoon, decided to figure out how to cross it tomorrow. I set up camp and ate dry again. After getting everything in order, I looked upstream and noticed patches of snow here and there with snowdrift on large boulders. A strong breeze blew my way and gave me a big chill as it crossed over the snow and into my body. I froze for a few seconds, rushed into my tent and stayed there till morning.

In the morning, I walked upstream to see if there were any large rocks on the river for an easier way to cross....there wasn't. There was a large Lodgepole tree that had fallen over the river and could be walked on as a bridge but was dangerous. If I would walk over it and fall into the river I would surely be swept away and drown. I thought about that raven that flew over me yesterday. I packed up my gear, put the backpack on my back and sat on the end of the snag. I then just started scooting a few inches at a time across that river. It took twenty minutes to get to the other side of the river but I was safe.

HOCKETT MEADOW

I was overjoyed that I made it over the river safely and there was no more climbing. I climbed 5,500 ft. in two days and now I'm walking level, for the most part, towards Hockett Lakes and beyond. As I walked down the trail, I noticed a large snag that fell beside the trail. As I got closer I realized there was a small triangle of sawdust beside it....but how, I thought, did that happen. When I reached it, I saw a flake of sawdust fall on the blond mound from a crack on the snag. There I saw, to my amazement, one carpenter ant after another dropping one flake at a time onto the mound below. It was absolutely amazing and I couldn't keep my eyes off of it. I smiled and marveled at the beauty of Mother Nature's little creatures working together to make their home inside the trunk of that snag. There must have been millions of flakes on that mound.

After meandering through the trail winding down towards Hockett Lakes, I heard birds singing for the first time in two days. I found a large granite boulder by one of the lakes, sat there and had a lunch of raisins, dates, and nuts. After an hour of eating, relaxing, and hearing a woodpecker attack a tree every couple of minutes, I continued on the trail. I soon came upon an open field with small Lodgepole trees spaced about twenty feet apart. Beyond that field, I saw a huge sand hill to my right. It looked like a small pyramid. I chose not to walk on top of it fearing that it might swallow me up. The trail forked just ahead of me with a sign that stated Hockett Meadow to the left and Southfork Junction to the right. I noticed horseshoe prints on the trail and remembered about the horse trailers I saw at the trailhead. Checking the direction of the horse party......they went right, so I went left.

I figured we were around 8,500 ft. and the trail was very level with lodgepole trees everywhere. As I was walking along, I heard a woodpecker pecking away. I turned to my right to find him but instead saw a big buck lying on the grass and keeping his eye on me. He was a four-pointer, as we call them in the West…..four points on one side of his antlers. I quietly pulled out my map and figured that just east of that buck was Mitchell Meadow but there was no trail to go there. There were large Lodgepoles all around me and after walking about 300 ft., the trail merged right where a small wooden bridge made of small logs covered Whitman Creek, which meanders from the north side of the meadow. Just beyond the bridge I saw some campsites and beyond that was a very well-made log cabin Ranger Station. It had a small front porch with railings facing south. There was a flag pole in the front yard and east of the station was a fence with wooden posts and barbed wire, four-strung horizontally to keep horses away from the station, I thought. There wasn't anyone around that I could see but since there was a horse within the enclosure, I figured maybe somebody was around. I yelled out, "Anybody there?". A man dressed in a second-class NPS uniform, which is the dress of maintenance and back-country Rangers, emerged. He had a long beard, in his 50's or 60's and seemed surprised to see me.
"Hi there…..didn't know anyone was here yet." the ranger said.
"I just came from Garfield Grove trail…..first time here." I said, with a big smile.
"Well, you are certainly welcome. Did you have a good hike?" he said as he walked towards me.

"Yes, thank you.....beautiful meadow here" as I looked at the length of it.

"My name is Harrison Hawk and I came to explore this great wilderness."

He smiled and said, "I was just getting to put on a horseshoe on my horse, but I'll take a break. Let's walk over here and get acquainted."

We walked to his porch. He had a rocking chair and he sat on it. I took my pack off and sat on the steps. I looked at his name tag.....I could see his first name was 'Leonardo'. He noticed me looking at it and said, "Just call me Leo."

"I'd like to camp here for a few nights, Leo." I said.

"Sure, glad to have you. There are campsites right next to us here and there's a real nice one on the east side of the meadow, if you want more privacy."

He pointed to it.

"Do you see that yellow marker on that lodgepole over there?"

"I do." I answered.

"That's 'Snow Marker Camp'.....usually horse campers go over there but it's empty right now."

I told him about the horse trailer and prints I saw on the trail.

"They're probably at Southfork Junction on the way to Windy Gap and Blossom Lakes area."

We chatted for about an hour and then I walked to Snow Marker Camp with my pack. It was a nice camp with a fire pit and a level area to pitch my tent. I could see the Ranger Station about 200 ft. to my right. My camp was situated right next to the meadow so, after putting my food in the bear box, I decided to walk the perimeter of the meadow. It was refreshing to see, hear, and feel the beauty of the wilderness. It made me feel so free. I wondered if any of my Yokut ancestors walked here many years ago. I had all kinds of images run through my mind about the area….how would it look with snow on it or with rain and thunder? I marveled at the beauty of this gorgeous meadow. As I came around the last section of the meadow, I saw the ranger getting on his horse and it looked like he was going on patrol. I decided to go back to camp and look for firewood. After eating my beef jerky and nuts, I made a fire, sat on a granite boulder and really started to enjoy this trip.

I dozed off and when I came to, I saw another backpacker pitching his tent next to the Ranger Station. I looked through my monocular and noticed he had a boy of about 15 years old with him…..maybe his son, I thought. I put out the fire and took my canteens and water filter to Whitman Creek, which flows and meanders through the meadow. There was a fence that divided the horse pasture with the Ranger Station. After filling up my canteens, I crossed over the fence and saw a large campsite with a fire pit and a half-cord of firewood nearby. There were large lodgepoles around the site which provided shade on sunny days. It was a great campsite so I called it 'The Hilton'. It was about 100 yards from the Ranger Station and there was a family of marmots looking at me, no doubt wondering what I was up to. Marmots are clever creatures. They make tunnels underground and usually around large granite boulders. They are in the squirrel family but look like beavers but without a webbed tail. They are golden in color, for the most part, and are very inquisitive, quiet, and like to place themselves on the highest boulder around to have a good view of the surroundings. A story

I heard from a ranger is that they like to chew on our vehicles water hoses and antifreeze hoses. The sweet smell of the antifreeze attracts them and it can be very distressing to backpackers when they return from a hike and realize they need a new hose. The best way to deter their damages is to surround the vehicle with chicken wire to solve that problem, but I love seeing them around in their natural habitat.

EVELYN LAKE

The next morning, I decided to take a hike to Evelyn Lake, which is about 2 miles northwest of the meadow. After eating breakfast, I put some food and water into my small daypack and checked my tent to make sure there were no aromatic items left behind or I might see my camp trashed by a bear when I returned.

As I hiked up the trail to the lake I started climbing on smooth granite rock with tiny lodgepole trees growing out of their cracks.....it's amazing how trees can do that.....the will to live, in Mother Nature's paradise. After hiking about a mile and a half the trail led me to this depression and looking below me, I could see Evelyn Lake. It was kind of hidden from sight with rock and lodgepoles surrounding it. It was a sunny day and warm enough to maybe take dip in that emerald-colored lake. I took off my pack near the edge of it and ran my fingers over the top of the water. It was nice and warm. I looked around and with no one in sight, I took off all my clothes and dove in head first. "Oh, my God.", I yelled out. I jumped out of the lake as fast as I could. I was shivering and quickly dried my body with a dry clean rag that I had in my pack. I put my clothes back on. Plunging into the lake was invigorating and woke me up with that cold burst to my body.

I took out my pen and paper and started to write down about my experiences of the trip. After writing for about twenty minutes, I heard a noise above me. I looked up and saw three horses with riders above me coming down towards the lake. I waved at them and I was glad they came after my skinny-dipping episode and not during it.

"Howdy, there.", the woman rider exclaimed. I guessed she was in her 40's.

There were two other men on their horses, also middle-aged. They got off their horses and came to talk with me.

"Beautiful little lake here" I said.

"Yes", one of the men said. "We always make a point of coming to see Evelyn when we're in the area."

"Where are you folks from?" I said with a smile.

"We have horses on our ranch in Woodlake so we come out here from time to time.", the woman said.

They were nice folks. They had lots of stories about their trips up here in the mountains. I enjoyed talking with them.

"Are you the ones that have a horse trailer I saw down by Southfork Campground?" I asked.

"That's us." The third man said.

"That's the best way to come up. Climbing 5,500 feet by foot is too tough." the woman said.

"It took me two days to get up here, so, yeah, you're right." I
said.
They laughed. I reached into my pack and pulled out the rope
bridle I found on the trail and handed it to the woman.
"I found this on the trail. I figured it was yours."
They thanked me and acknowledged that it was theirs.
I put on my backpack and wished them good luck. I started up
the trail and about halfway up that depression I heard a splash. I
looked back and noticed that the woman and one of the men
jumped in the lake. They were yelling and splashing water on
each other and having a good time. I wondered if they were
skinny-dipping but noticed they both had swimming suits on. I
thought how great it was to see people enjoying themselves
here in this mountain paradise. As
I was walking back to camp the sun was shining and there was a
slight breeze caressing my face. I looked up to the sky and heard
the raven cry out. I wondered if it was the same one that I saw
at the grove.....couldn't be.....or could it?

As I walked back to camp, I noticed bear tracks on the
ground. I wondered if the raven was warning me about
something. I looked around me but didn't see any bears but still
walked back to camp as quietly as possible.

CAHOON ROCK

I stayed at Hockett Meadow a few more nights and took
day hikes to get acquainted with the area. I would spend the

early evenings chatting with Leo until twilight time. After getting a good night's sleep I broke camp, put all my gear in my backpack and walked to the Ranger Station. Leo was sitting on his rocking chair smoking his pipe. I greeted him and told him I was leaving.

"I plan to go back to Southfork Campground by way of an old pioneers trail that starts out from Cahoon Rock and goes through the base of Homers Nose."

"That trail is not maintained and is a bit dangerous with some steep areas." he said.

"Well, I plan to go slow and being careful." I responded.

"If you have any problems just make sure you keep the Southfork River in sight and you should be OK." he warned.

DEAD MAN'S TRAIL

We said our goodbyes and off I went toward Cahoon Rock. It was the same trail that I took to Evelyn Lake but forks up ahead where I'll take a left instead of a right that goes to Evelyn. I heard that raven again but didn't bother looking up to find him. After a quarter mile or so I was on the Rock. There was a great view of the wilderness and straight ahead I could see Homers Nose. I started looking for that old trail but nothing looked like a definite trail. I remember Leo saying that it wasn't maintained so I figured it would look narrow and overgrown with plants. As I looked all over the area, I saw one that looked like a trail at one time and it was a bit steep going down but I was pretty sure that it was the one I was looking for so I started down that trail. The raven, perched on a lodgepole tree branch started cawing again.

After hiking down about thirty or forty yards, the trail seemed to disappear in front of a deer brush area. That's when I realized that the trail was not a trail at all.....it was a water drainage. I started to walk back up the steep mountain but my boots would sink halfway into the granite pebbles. My heavy backpack made it even worse by dragging me down. I had to make a decision whether to continue to climb on all fours or take a chance and follow the river, as Leo recommended. I turned around and looked down towards the river which was about 5,000 feet below. I decided to chance it and keep going down. I heard the raven cawing again over and over and over again. For the first time since I started the trip, I felt fear knowing I was going down the mountain in a way that no one had done before. I felt like cursing my ancestors for thinking a raven could foresee danger ahead, after all, I was an educated man and I will not be superstitious like my ancestors were.

I built up my courage and continued to move down any possible way I could. I tore through the manzanita brush which was so hard to do. The rock-hard branches were scratching my arms and legs. I noticed the skin on my left arm was bleeding. I turned around and let my backpack hit the branches first and lead me through to the next patch of vegetation. It started getting very steep so I had to drop my body and slide down the loose soil but as I was sliding down I noticed a wide slab of granite ahead of me and beyond it was a huge drop of about 100 feet. I quickly turned onto my belly and, still sliding, I couldn't stop myself. I knew I was going down possibly to my death. Just before I came to the edge of the cliff, I looked to my right and saw a tiny manzanita plant growing out from a crack of the huge granite slab. I grabbed it with my right hand. It stopped me from sliding, since manzanita plants are extremely tough. I stayed motionless for what seemed like eternity, breathing so hard and clutching the plant with all my might. I slowly started inching my body towards my right until I could reach a bigger manzanita branch. Inch by inch I moved sideways to the edge of the granite slab and realized I was finally out of danger. My body was shaking and my arms were tight with muscles twitching from the isometrics. I couldn't move and I passed out.

I woke up and noticed it was twilight time. It will soon be pitch dark and here I was lying on a fifty-degree slope where it was impossible to even stand up. While still lying on the ground, I took out my sleeping bag and spread it out next to me. I started to slip down as I was working it so I had to move very slow and unzip it. It took awhile to finally unzip the bag. I couldn't get inside of it or I would slide down into some pine trees below me. I felt so cold now that the sun had gone down. I stayed lying on the soil and positioned the sleeping bag over me. I used my backpack as a pillow. I could smell my food from that ripped area of my pack. I thought if I could smell it, a bear surely can too and I could not protect myself or even try to shoo him away. I felt so helpless in this perilous descent until I remembered what my great grandfather said, "…pray to the Great Spirit and He will help you." I prayed and prayed until I finally fell asleep.

I woke up in the middle of the night to a bright light shining on me. I thought someone had found me and everything will be all right now. I was lying on my stomach so I couldn't see anyone and wouldn't try to move or I might start sliding down again. I yelled out….."Here I am….I'm here….I'm alive…here." There was silence. I turned my head from side to side and noticed the light was shining all over the area. I slowly turned over and realized the light was from a full moon shining so bright on a clear, cold night. There were a trillion stars in the sky. I could see them even with a full moon that illuminated the quiet forest. The stars looked so beautiful but I was still so cold. I reached inside my pack for my knit cap and another sweater but any movement made me slide four or five inches down the steep granite slab. I curled myself into a ball and fell asleep again.

In the early morning I had a better view of my surroundings. I rolled up my sleeping bag and with one hand tied it to the outside of my backpack. I was able to sit up and see how I could continue. I noticed a brushy area to my left and if I could scoot sideways to where it could be directly below me, I could drop myself into the brush, since it was only about a fifteen-foot drop. It took about an hour to get myself into position for a safe drop. I dropped my backpack onto the brush first and I started the slide slowly and slid down and fell on my backpack. It cushioned the fall and now I found myself in a less steep area with trees all around me. I could finally stand up. I put my pack on my back and started descending downwards towards the river below. The trees were obscuring the river but I knew it was down there somewhere. After going down for an hour or so, I was relieved to see a small plateau just below me. I got excited and moved faster towards it.

When I reached the plateau, I collapsed. My legs were in such pain because of the braking I had to do while coming down on such steep terrain. I lay down for an hour to rest. I then checked my pack and noticed I dropped something from that hole that the manzanita branches tore into. It was my small stove and fuel that were in a bag. So, they were up there somewhere on the mountain. Luckily, my food was still there and I had one liter of water left in my bag. I grabbed some beef jerky, nuts, and water canteen and feasted on that.

At the edge of the plateau I noticed more manzanita patches below me so I looked for another area to continue my descent. My legs were still killing me but I had to fight it or I'd have to spend another freezing night on the mountain. I didn't want to pitch my tent and spend the night. I figured I was about halfway down the mountain and wanted to reach the river before nightfall.

WHISKEY LOG CAMP

I slid down the mountain step by step for two hours stumbling through deer brush and around trees. I noticed that now I'm see white fir trees instead of red fir trees, which made me glad that I'm getting closer and closer to the river. I saw a big Cedar tree and stopped there to eat the rest of my jerky and nuts, took a sip from my canteen but saved the last cup or so for later. After eating I rubbed my knees, which were giving me a lot of pain. They were screaming for me to stop walking but I had to move on.

I saw some dead snags below me with mushroom fungi growing on them. They were bright yellow and as big as a small loaf of bread, which made me hungry. I soon came upon a big slab of granite that I could walk on towards another stand of white firs up ahead. As I walked through it, I thought I heard something. I stopped and listened carefully. It sounded like a motor or some kind of generator. I got excited and walked faster and faster. The sound became louder and louder and I realized it was the sound of the river below me. My heart started beating faster and faster and I didn't think about the pain in my knees.

As I raced down as fast as I could I was thrilled to see a campsite down below. It had a fire pit and right there and then I knew I made it. I didn't know where I was until I took out my map and realized it was Whiskey Log Camp. I rested in the campsite for an hour and a half then continued down a real trail, not a water drainage. I felt exalted in knowing that I would be safe and be home soon. The trail was a bit dangerous in spots but I laughed when I thought of it, after what I've been through for two days.

I continued on down as the river sounded louder and louder. After some switchbacks, I came down onto another wide trail. I could now see the river clearly and I thanked God for getting me back safe. I walked down the trail and came to another campground called Ladybug Camp. I didn't walk down to the campsites to check them out. I just wanted to get back home as soon as I could. After another mile and a half, I reached Southfork Campground. The horse trailers were still there. I dragged myself to the first campsite I saw. I looked to my right and there was a family of four laughing and eating dinner over a fire. It looked like a perfect setting for a family camping experience.

I then heard a raven cawing and flying overhead. I raised my fist up in the air and I laughed out loud. The family looked at me and probably thought I was crazy.

Harrison Hawk

Sequoia Mountain Man

(a book of Adventures in the Wild – episode 2)

By

Connor Corkill

SEQUOIA NATIONAL PARK

PABLO

As I walked past the front gate of my great grandpa's house, I noticed a motorcycle parked on his front lawn. It was an old Harley Davidson with a hawk painted on the gas tank. The Spanish word for horse, "Caballo", was hand-painted on the frame, and red-tailed hawk feathers were hanging from the handlebars. I knocked on the front door then peeked through the window and saw the silhouette of a long-haired man answering the door. I knew who it was.

"Hello, Harry", he said, as he opened the door. It was my older step-brother, Pablo Hawk. He was the son of my dad, Benjamin, who was married to a Mexican woman. She died giving birth to Pablo. My dad married my mother two years later.

 "It's good to see you again, brother", I said.

We embraced with a hug and quick kiss on the cheek. We walked to the old sofa with Little Red Hawk, our great grandpa. I told them the whole story of my first solo backpack trip and how I made the mistake of taking the wrong path.

"Don't be disappointed, my son", Papo said. "the raven you saw and then heard him 'caw' in that early morning, may have been a warning that something bad might happen but as you kept seeing him following you along, he was letting you know that he is watching over you because you made a mistake. If you don't make mistakes, you'll never improve. That's how you learn and ……

 "If you would have known what I have studied, you would not have made that mistake.", Pablo interrupted.

My brother had been studying the teachings of Don Juan, a "shaman", that teaches the philosophies of Indian and Mexican culture with herbal medicines derived from peyote, a hallucinogenic plant. In the past, my brother had tried to recruit me into this ideology but I didn't want to take any drugs that would impair my mind. My brother said that it would open the mind and make you more aware of the basic mediums of human existence.

"Listen to your brother. He can help you to see the mountains in a different way…. a way of the shaman.", the old man said.

"I just want to see, hear, and feel the Sierra Nevada mountains as our ancestors did two hundred years ago……. I feel like I need that knowledge." I said.

"Let's go to Giant Forest…. there you'll be able to understand what I mean." Pablo replied.

We said our goodbyes to our grandpa and walked out the door. Pablo mounted his "Caballo" and I sat behind him. Waving goodbye, we rumbled away towards Sequoia National Park. After going through the entrance station, we continued on past the "Indian Head" then the Ash Mountain Visitor Center, where we stopped for a 'Tom Harrison' map, which gives us great color and 'mileage' between certain points…. also, a 'Trails Illustrated' map which is best for topography readings.

As we entered Giant Forest, we saw a raven. He cried out to us. My brother looked at me and slowly nodded.

Giant Forest

We rolled into Giant Forest, turned left into the parking lot, parked the "Caballo" and walked down the steps towards the Highway. Before us was the great "Sentinel" Giant Sequoia tree. There were many people staring at the great giant. It is right in front of the Giant Forest Museum, which has all information that one needs to understand the beauty of how the tiniest of seeds can grow to such a huge giant.

There are seventy-five locations of Giant Sequoia stands and Giant Forest has four of the five largest Giant Sequoias. Within the three-square miles of Giant Forest there are almost forty miles of trails with meadows containing lush flower-filled plants and, if you're lucky, you'll see a mother bear and her cub feasting on berries.

We hiked the perimeter of those beautiful meadows, including Hazelwood Nature Trail, Huckleberry Meadow Loop, and Crescent Meadow, which is next to the trailhead of the High Sierra Trail, a 72-mile trail that ends on top of Mt. Whitney on the east side of the Sierra Nevada mountains.

As we walked back to the parking lot, Pablo stopped and said,

"According to a Yokut tradition, our hiking ancestors were given special blessings from the elders before they would embark on journeys to the High Sierras. I am not an elder but I will take you to four special places that are part of those prayers and we will say prayers together.".

General Sherman Tree

Pablo told me that to see the great mountains of the Sierras, we should prepare ourselves mentally as well as physically, for there are many dangers that will await us. But we can train our mind to withstand the difficulties that Mother Nature will bestow upon us.

We mounted the bike and drove about four miles down Generals Highway. We parked and walked to the giant. It was absolutely enormous…..the largest tree in the world…..amazing. I looked up and noticed that the branches alone where big enough to be very large trees down here on the ground.

Pablo chose a grassy, level area where we could sit and view the giant. We sat on the ground with crossed legs, back straight, eyes closed, and Pablo started reciting a Yokut prayer that I was not familiar with.

The first prayer of a Yokut Indian before he ventures into the mountains has a special meaning. It is the same as when our great grandfather was born and his parents saw a little Hawk fly by therefore naming him 'Little Hawk'.

"This prayer that I prayed is before the largest tree on earth, so I will call you 'Sequoia Mountain Man'. Come.....there is more to see" Pablo said.

Tocopah Falls

We walked back to the parking lot and drove the "Caballo" to Lodgepole Campground, which is about 5 miles north of the Giant Forest Museum. We crossed the wooden bridge over Marble Fork of the Kaweah River and there before us was the trailhead to Tocopah Falls, only 1.7 miles away. Deer, squirrels, and marmots are seen along the gradual uphill trail that leads to the 1,200 ft. high Falls. Lodgepole trees were the most plentiful as we hiked upstream for most of the way. The soft litter of organic matter beneath our feet soon felt the cold, hardness of granite as we were now in alpine area.

Pablo and I sat on a large granite boulder and watched the power of the water coming down the falls. We positioned ourselves in the previous 'prayer mode' as Pablo recited the prayer and added a chant that lasted a few minutes

Pablo finally spoke...."Water is the most precious element you must have. It will give you life but it can also take away your life. You must treat all of Mother Nature's powers with respect."

We walked back to the campground parking lot, mounted the bike and drove to the next destination, of which I knew nothing about. We passed Giant Forest and drove up the road towards Crescent Meadow. We stopped at the base of Moro Rock and parked alongside other vehicles.

Moro Rock

We climbed the concrete and stone stairway to the top of Moro Rock. There are handrails to help folks up the 350 steps. It was a clear, and calm day. The gentle breeze felt good after a hard climb. Pablo grabbed my hand and raised it high. He started chanting in Yokut language. I had no idea what he was saying....I just closed my eyes and waited for him to finish his prayer. Pablo released my hand, slowly turned to look at me, smiled and nodded.

"Air is necessary for life but if it moves too fast, the wind can also take away your life. Be mindful of the power of wind, rain, hail, snow, which are all Mother Nature's children.....respect them."

I realized now that Pablo was a wiser man than I thought. He has certainly read literature on respecting the land we live in. I am learning from my brother and I am glad he brought me here with him.

As we walked down the stairs, I realized how easy it is to make one mistake and die from it, like I almost did on my first solo backpacking trip. I am learning and will keep learning.

SUNSET ROCK

We drove back to the Giant Forest Museum parking lot. It was late afternoon now and it will soon be twilight. We walked to Sunset Rock, which is a huge slab of concrete and perfect for seeing the sunset. We walked on the slab and saw a depression with smooth sand. We made a small fire and sat around it. The sun was setting and it changed the color of the sky from blue to lavender to gold as we sat and, as if in a trance, stared at the sun until it set.

"The sun gives us warmth and helps to grow our plant food. Without it, humans will die but it also gives us life. Some people worship the sun because if it's life-giving properties. Pray to the Holy Spirit for strength as you go to the highest mountains." Pablo prayed.

We stood up and walked back to the parking lot at twilight time. A raven was perched on a pine tree............ waiting for us to leave so he can fly down and eat the nuts I left for him.

Harrison Hawk

Sequoia Mountain Man

a book of Adventures in the Wild – episode 3)

by

Connor Corkill

S.N.P.-S.N.F. LOOP

TWIN LAKES TRAIL

The Twin Lakes Trail starts in Lodgepole Campground. The excitement of waiting many months to backpack again has reached its peak. The month of June in Sequoia National Park still has snow patches at 6,000 feet. My brother, Pablo, worked as a guide for the Indian Conservancy Organization in the Tule area. He was free for two weeks so I asked him to join me on my backpack trip.

We started on the trailhead of Twin Lakes Trail, which is only twenty yards away from the Tocopah Falls trailhead. It is very steep with granite rocks protruding out of the rich organic topsoil that dead lodgepole trees create as they break down over centuries. The trail runs parallel to the Lodgepole Campground for the first mile where we stopped. I looked back at the Lodgepole Valley.

"Pablo, did you know that this gorgeous valley was filled with hundreds of feet of glacial ice about 10,000 years ago?" I said.
"No humans could survive here at that time" he answered.
"Our ancestors walked this valley but only a few thousand years ago, I suspect." I said.
We continued our climb. The moraine we were on consisted of a mixed vegetation of manzanita and many pine and cedar trees. The forest was blocking the morning sunlight and only hints of sunrays were shining thru from the high canopy above us. Soon we were approaching a large meadow on our left. It was Cahoon Meadow, according to my map. We were hoping to see a bear and cub devouring berries but we weren't lucky.
On and on we climbed and eventually reached Cahoon Gap, which was about 8,700 ft. elevation.
"Let's take a break....I'm tired" Pablo said.
"Yes, I want to check the map anyway." I said, as we looked for a place to sit.
The Gap had opened up with about thirty-feet spacing from tree to tree. I checked the topography on the map.
"It's all down slope to our first camp, which is Clover Creek." I stated.
"Good. I'm getting hungry." Pablo said, as he sighed in relief.
We continued on and we heard the sound of water flowing. We then saw Clover Creek and soon two campsites.
There was no one around so we chose the best campsite, took our packs off and pitched our tents. We hung our food from two pine tree branches and looked for firewood. The creek had plenty of water for us to fill our canteens.
We made a fire and heated our water for some pasta for dinner. After dinner, we both went to bed early, since we were very tired from climbing with our heavy backpacks.

JENNY LAKE

We woke up at dawn. It was cold and there was a foggy mist around our camp. We immediately started a fire to warm ourselves up, got our stoves, filled them with water and heated them to a boil for our coffee and oatmeal breakfast. After we ate and packed our supplies into our backpack, I looked at our map.

My original plan was to go to Twin Lakes, which was only two miles away. It was   all uphill but Pablo wanted to see Jenny Lake.

"If we go to Jenny Lake, we would have to leave Sequoia National Park and cross over to Sequoia National Forest." I reminded him.

"I heard that lake has great fishing…….big fish. We can have a really good fresh trout dinner tonight". Pablo said.

The sound of fresh trout for dinner convinced me of going there too so off we went.

We climbed about one thousand feet, passing ferns and dense vegetation under pine trees and then open areas back and forth. After climbing 600 feet or so, I looked to my right at an open field and saw Mt. Silliman, with its scattered snow patches near the top of the peak. We continued on and came upon a shady plateau with fir trees all around, which was a welcome site after hiking in the open area where the sun was bearing down on us with its eighty-degree heat.

At last we could see the top of the ridge where there was supposed to be a marker that said, "JO". It was carved into a pine tree maybe a hundred years ago, they say, by a pioneer who wanted to carve out "JOHN", which was his name but, I guess got tired after the "O". Anyway, it was a welcome sight. We stopped there to rest. Next to a boulder was a sign that marked the boundary line from Sequoia National Park into Sequoia National Forest. We didn't continue on the trail to the north. We made a left turn towards the west toward Jenny Lake. The trail climbed for a hundred feet then dropped for another hundred or so. That happened a few times until we reached Jenny Lake. It was a beautiful little lake….very quiet. We didn't notice any other hikers or campers. We chose the first campsite we saw, which happened to be the best one because it had both shade and sunshine. It was next to the outlet of the lake and we chose our tent spots, pitched our tents, put our food in the bear box and rested for a half hour or so before making our dinner. We were too tired to look for wood for our fire pit so we ate dry and being that it was near dusk, we turned in and soon fell asleep.

ROCKSLIDE

When we woke up, it was sunny and cool. Pablo and I dragged ourselves out of our sleeping bags and after lighting up our stove, we boiled our water and made coffee. After a breakfast of our usual oatmeal and biscuits, we locked up our food and explored the area. There were more campsites and some good ones up on a hill. As we were sitting on a large boulder, we heard what we thought was an airplane's motor getting louder and louder. We ducked thinking the plane was crashing into our area. My heart was beating fast, expecting a huge crash. The sound subsided as we looked across the lake and we saw a large cloud of dust and medium-sized boulders rolling down the cliff. We realized that the sound we heard was a rockslide. There were more boulders and soil rolling down into the far side of the lake, which made ripples of water rolling toward our side of the lake. We couldn't believe it. On our first layover day, we witnessed the ending of a rockslide.

"Unbelieveable" I said.

"Yes, Mother Nature is talking to us" Pablo said.

We walked by the edge of the lake and gathered some firewood and returned to camp. Pablo opened his backpack and pulled out his fishing kit of telescopic rod, small hooks, fishing line and walked to the shore.

"I'm hoping to catch some trout for our dinner, brother" he said. I stayed in camp and was studying a map when, after about 2 hours, he walked back with five large trout on a fishing line.

"We've got dinner" he said with a big smile on his face.

He pulled out a frying pan and a small bottle of oil and, after scaling the fish and cleaning them, started frying them on our small propane stove. We made a fire and wrapped two potatoes with foil paper and placed them by the edge of the firepit. After thirty minutes or so, we were enjoying the best fish and potato dinner I've had in many years.

The next morning, after breakfast, we headed back to 'JO' Pass and continued on in Sequoia National Forest toward Rowell Meadow. The trail was fairly straight with Red Fir trees mixed with Lodgepoles and we walked on granite slabs. Rain clouds were forming and soon it started sprinkling. We increased our pace hoping to make it to our next campsite in Rowell Meadow. There was a large snag to our left with a Goshawk perched on a dead branch. We kept our eye on it, since that species of raptor will attack if we are too close to their nest. The rain clouds moved on away from us and we finally reached our destination……Rowell Meadow

ROWELL MEADOW

As we rolled in, we saw the cabin and we hurried toward it. It started sprinkling again but a little harder. We tried to enter from the front door, since we noticed no one was around. It started raining harder and harder. Pablo went to the side of the cabin and noticed that he could unscrew the bolts of the wooden window frame. He took it down and we jumped in just as the rain started pouring down. It was dark inside but we were mostly dry except for our jackets. We took them off and hung them on spikes that were nailed into the 6 x 6 posts. With our flashlights scanning the interior, we saw 8 frying pans nailed to one wall. Each one had a name to it…."Bob", another "Jim", etc.. We figured they were park rangers or fire crew members that would stay here from time to time. There were some cans of beans and corn but we didn't touch them. We pulled out our beef jerky, water canteens, ate dinner and enjoyed the sound of the rain.

In the morning, the rain stopped and we crawled out through the window. There were many puddles of water everywhere but we had blue skies. We were almost out of drinking water so we looked for a creek, or a brook to fill our canteens. We didn't find anything so we continued on the trail which will take us back into the Sequoia National Park. As we were walking, we noticed a man and a woman in a campsite. I waved at them and they waved back but no words were exchanged. The trail was pretty easy…..a hill here and there but, for the most part, was enjoyable. We soon saw the sign, "Entering Sequoia National Park". There was a big dip on the trail as we continued then we climbed up a hill. Soon we were entering an open fern forest on the trail. We eventually came to a fork where, if we go left, we will head towards Roaring River and if we go right, Seville Lake. We went right.

SEVILLE LAKE

After walking about a half mile, there was another fork on the trail with a sign that said Seville Lake. We were surprised that we hadn't seen any wildlife since that Goshawk yesterday morning. As we entered the lakes entrance, we saw four young men camped on a campsite near the lake. They seemed to be in good spirits, laughing and talking with each other. Pablo and I went to talk to them, since they looked very friendly. We found out they were musicians of a Latin-Jazz group from Los Angeles. They had a cassette player and played jazz music. It's a good thing no other backpackers were camped at the lake or they might have complained about the noise. Pablo and I loved music so we chatted for a while then walked around the north side of the lake to have more privacy. We found a good, secluded campsite and pitched our tents. There was a bear box for our food. We heated our water and had pasta with spices for dinner. Tired from our hike, we turned in and fell asleep right away.

When the sun hit my tent, I woke up, started a fire in our firepit and boiled some water for our coffee. The smell of hot coffee woke up my bro and we ate our breakfast.
"Are you going to fish today?" I asked.
"No, I'm having strange vibes about this place. I think we should move on after breakfast." Pablo answered.

"What do you mean by that?" I wondered.
"I'm not sure....maybe because of a bad dream I had last night.
I'll tell you about it later."
I didn't press him to tell me about the dream. I just agreed to
pack up and leave as soon as possible. As we started to walk out
with our packs, we noticed the jazz band members were gone.
They must have left very early in the morning. I wondered if
they had anything to do with Pablo's dream that maybe spelled
a bad omen for us. Pablo was getting a little paranoid for some
reason.
I didn't ask for more information and wondered if we really saw
those guys last night or if they were ghosts and not real at all. I
felt a strange chill and just wanted to walk faster and get away
from Seville Lake. Now I was getting paranoid.

RANGER LAKE

As we walked into Ranger Lake, we noticed a small island on the
far side of the lake. We walked around to that area since it
looked more private and away from the trail. There were many
lodgepole and red fir trees around it. We found a nice, secluded
campsite. It was the farthest one away from the trail. We
pitched our tents, hung our food and, with our bathing suits,
jumped into the water for a swim. It was cold but very
refreshing. We swam around for a half hour or so and walked
back to camp.

THE WOLF

"Are you going to tell me about your dream now?" I asked.
"It was a strange dream......about the Raven....like something bad might happen." he said.
"This looks like paradise here. Nothing bad will happen. We haven't seen any bears or wildlife besides the birds." I said.
"Well, I hope it was nothing." he muttered.
We looked for some firewood and made a fire in the existing firepit. We ate nuts and dried fruit and talked about the fun times we had as kids together. As dusk was approaching, we thought we heard a wolf howling. Our eyes lit up.
"What was that?" I exclaimed.
"Sounded like a wolf" Pablo said as he stood up and looked around.
"There aren't any wolves in this park. They're all up north." I said.
"Yeah, well, it sure sounded like a wolf." Pablo said as he looked all around the camp.
We put out the fire and got in our sleeping bags. We heard the howling sounds again. I stuck my head out of the tent, looked up on the hill and saw the silhouette of a large wolf walking slowly about forty yards away from us. The moon was not full but the half-moon gave enough light to shine on our camp. I looked to my left and Pablo was standing near his tent staring at the wolf.
"Pablo.....did you see him?" I whispered.
"Yes, he is a big one alright but he disappeared around the pines." He replied.
We waited outside our tents to see if he would come out again. Our food was safe in a bear box but it was getting cold so we got back in our tents and eventually fell asleep.
        The next morning, I peeked out of my tent. Pablo had already started a fire in the pit. He got our food out of the bear

box and started boiling water for our coffee and oatmeal. I dragged myself out of the tent and walked up to him.

"Did you see him again?" I asked.

"No" he answered.

"At first I thought I was dreaming but he looked real." I said.

"Yes, but I was reading this pamphlet about the area and there are definitely no wolves here so he must have a been a very big coyote." Pablo stated.

"Well, he knows we're here and I don't want to spend another night here." I said.

"Yes, we'll go over Silliman Pass today to Twin Lakes and go home." Pablo said.

As we walked out in the morning, we saw a beautiful scenery of Mt. Silliman as the backdrop of this beautiful lake. I took a picture and we hiked out.

TWIN LAKES

The trail to Silliman Pass was not bad at all. We climbed on granite switchbacks. When we got to the Pass, we looked east and saw a beautiful view of the mountains that were beyond the Kern River. We also saw the Twin Peaks near us but decided to continue on to Twin Lakes. We descended with more switchbacks until we got to the first lake. There were many great campsites. We took our backpacks off and sat on a downed snag. We ate more nuts and most of our beef jerky. We noticed a woman looking up at the Twin Peaks with binoculars. I asked her what she was looking at and she said her boyfriend was climbing the Peaks but she couldn't find him. They were from Germany but she spoke English. I wished her luck and we started to hike out of the lakes. As we walked to the far side of the lake, we saw two women and a man swimming in the lake. As they came out of the water, both women were completely naked. Pablo and I decided to enjoy the view for a while. After they came out and got dressed, they walked past us on their way to Silliman Pass. We asked them where they were from and they said that they were from Sweden. They were very nice and we all continued on to our opposite destinations.

As we walked down the mountain, I almost stepped on a Rubber boa curled around the edge of the trail. It was of a brownish color and being a constrictor, it was harmless to humans. We smiled and agreed that we finally saw more wildlife since the "wolf" we saw at Ranger Lake.

We finally came to the point where we crossed the Twin Lakes trail to the JO trail. It was a great loop that we made and we decided to hike all the way back to Lodgepole. When we got there, we went to the grocery store and Pablo and I shared a six-pack of beer and ate sandwiches. It was a wonderful adventure that I'll never forget. As we sat by the river, drinking our beer, we saw a Steller Jay flying over us and landing on a pine branch....hoping I would share some of my sandwich with him, I thought. We laughed and threw him the last of our nuts, which he promptly picked up and flew away.

Harrison Hawk

Sequoia Mountain Man

(a book of Adventures in the Wild – episode 4)

by

Connor Corkill

THE LAKES TRAIL

THE WATCHTOWER

When my brother took me to see Tocopah Falls, we saw the beautiful cascade effect as the rush of water crashed on the granite floor. He said that the Watchtower, 1,600 feet above us, would be a challenge for me and the trail would take me to the Tablelands. So, from the Lodgepole area, I went to the trailhead located at the Wolverton parking lot. My brother, Pablo, had to work so I will be backpacking solo. The trail started gradually upward and increased in elevation gain quickly through gravel and topsoil ridges. These ridges were formed millions of years ago by the Tocopah Glacier. After hiking one mile on the Lakes Trail, it shifted south among the red fir trees.

After hiking 1.7 miles, I came to a trail junction. If I would continue straight upward, I would go over the Hump Trail, which was steep. I decided to go left towards the Watchtower route, which was more gradual but more dangerous if not careful. The trail hugged the cliff and I could see the Tocopah Falls and the Tocopah Valley below me. I tried to keep my eyes on the eight-feet wide trail and not get dizzy and fall 1,600 feet to my death. I was relieved that no one was hiking towards me or we'd have to carefully maneuver our way around each other.

After passing the dangerous trail, it coincided with the Hump Trail. I soon reached Heather Lake. It was a beautiful lake but I didn't see a campsite around it. I continued on and hoped that the next lake would have good campsites.

EMERALD LAKE

After a short climb, I looked to my left and saw a gorgeous little lake called Aster Lake in the Emerald Canyon. I didn't see any camping sites with my monocular so it must be for day use only, I thought. I walked down a gentle slope and came to Emerald Lake and there were many campsites there. I chose one that was very flat and near the outlet of the lake for me to fill my canteens. I pitched my tent and secured my food and supplies carefully. I didn't see any campers. I walked up toward the granite peaks behind me and there was the lake, with a strikingly beautiful green color. I sat on a granite boulder and had my lunch of nuts, dried fruit and water. The granite peaks behind the lake were creamy-white, as the sun shone directly into them. After eating my lunch, I decided to meditate and think about what my brother taught me regarding love and respect for nature. I was in complete silence for about a half hour until I heard someone speak.

"Hello there, camper" the voice yelled out.

I turned around from a serene mood to see a park ranger coming towards me.

"Hi" I said in a quiet voice.

"I noticed your tent and came to welcome you to Emerald Lake." The park ranger was a woman and she had a friendly look on her smiling face.

"I was relaxing and having my lunch." I said.

"Sorry to bother you. It's my job to check on visitors." she said. We talked for a while and she told me she stayed at Pear Lake Ski Hut Ranger Station, which was on the way to Pear Lake. The name tag on her uniform said "Christina..." I couldn't make out her last name. She was very nice and after twenty minutes or so, left to see if there were other campers.

I went back to my camp and started my dinner. The wind started blowing a bit harder as the sun was going down. Fires are not allowed that high in elevation so I retired into my tent after eating Ramen noodles for dinner.

The next morning, I noticed grey clouds moving very fast over me. I wondered if a storm was brewing. I quickly drank my coffee and ate my breakfast then packed up to go to Pear Lake before the rain would hit me. I didn't see any other campers at Emerald and I wanted to hurry and find a camp at Pear Lake. I hiked on the trail and came to a fork where going left would take me to the Ski Hut Ranger Station and taking a right would go to Pear Lake. I went right.

PEAR LAKE

I walked towards the lake with white granite peaks all around it. It was a large lake with a few trees growing out of the cracks so there wasn't much shade for any campers. I walked around to find the biggest tree and found one next to the well-made wooden restroom up on a large slab of granite. I looked up and was glad to see that the grey clouds were moving away and the sun was shining on the lake. I was lucky that there was a small shady tree next to my camp.

As I sat on a log, I noticed a tiny little chipmunk coming out of an opening at the base of my shady tree and was scampering around as fast as he could go. Soon a larger chipmunk came out and got on top of a small boulder and stood up on his hind legs as if to look for the little guy. Then another large chipmunk appeared at the opening and started making "chips and chuck sounds" as if giving the other large chipmunk instructions. I figured they were "Mom & Pop" looking for "Junior". I had a good time looking at these rodents living their lives almost like some humans do, i.e., parents looking after their children. It looked like "Pop" went after "Junior" and chased him back into the tree and I then heard "chip, chip, chip" sounds as if they were scolding "Junior" for running out without permission.

I walked towards the lake and noticed a man and a teenage boy fishing on the far side of the lake. I wondered if I will ever have a son and teach him to fish and hike with me. I thought about my ancestors walking these smooth flat granite rocks surrounding this beautiful lake and now I am here witnessing the same exact scenes that they saw. There is no change to how these mountains look for centuries, so I'm sure my ancestors saw them just as I'm seeing them now.

METEOR SHOWER

"Hello, again" I heard a female voice say.
It was Christina, the park ranger, who walked toward my campsite.
"Hi, Christina, good to see you again." I said.
"There is a Perseid meteor shower in full effect tonight. It happens every August so two friends and I are walking to Moose Lake at dusk, take our sleeping bags and see the meteors tonight. You're welcome to join us." she said.
"Wow….I didn't know about that. Yes, I'll go with you tonight. I was planning to see the tablelands tomorrow but to see a meteor shower tonight will be even more exciting." I said
"I'll meet you at my ranger station at dusk. Bring your jacket and a sleeping bag." she said.

MOOSE LAKE

As I walked up to Christina's ranger station late afternoon, there were two other people standing next to her. They weren't in uniform but neither was Christina. She told me they were park rangers too and it was their day off so they were in jeans and parkas and each carrying their sleeping bag tied to their day pack.

"Glad you could make it." Christina said.

She introduced me to her friends and we started the climb of solid granite towards the tablelands. We passed small lakes along the way to Moose Lake. Christina told me that there were many more dips of smooth granite on the tablelands creating smaller lakes. As we climbed a ridge and reached the top, we saw Moose Lake. It was huge and completely surrounded by granite, like Pear Lake, and no vegetation around it at all. Everyone chose their spot to lie down and laid out their sleeping bags while the cool wind blew past us during this twilight time. Before we got into our sleeping bags, there were meteors already visible shooting across the sky. The darker it got, the more visible the meteors shone above us, leaving streaks of ice crystals as they glowed across the sky. They seemed so close that we could touch them.

One of the rangers took out a pint of brandy and we all shared it, chasing it down with our canteens of water. After an hour or so the wind started blowing harder and colder. We decided that it was time to go back to our camps. We rolled up our sleeping bags and turned on our flashlights, even though the brightness of the meteor showers would shine on the granite rock and looked like a strobe light of nature. I'm glad we got back to the ranger station with just our flashlights. It was a very exciting evening. The wind started blowing harder and harder as I was trying to sleep with light flashes on the roof of my tent from the meteor shower but soon fell asleep.

The morning sun hit my tent early since there was no tree shade coming from the east. I made coffee and breakfast and just wanted to relax on this layover day. I was thinking of going up to the tablelands again and see it in the daylight but decided once was enough, since I knew the sun would be bearing down on me and there would be no place for shade. I marveled at Pear Lake and thanked God for such a beautiful paradise. I looked for that man and his son but I guess they left early in the morning. I walked around the lake and thought about jumping in for a cool dip but I started seeing other campers walking in and looking for a site.

The next morning, I packed up and walked down the mountain and felt good that there were no problems of any kind on this trip. I felt stronger than I had before I started the hike and felt that I could backpack anywhere else in the Sierra Nevada mountains without a problem, if I was careful. I was looking forward to my next adventure in September.

Harrison Hawk

Sequoia Mountain Man

(a book of Adventures in the Wild – episode 5)

By

Connor Corkill

RAE LAKES LOOP

UPPER PARADISE VALLEY

I needed a ride to Cedar Grove and I thought about Nick, who drove me to the Southfork Campground trailhead two years ago. I called him and he told me he would take me to Kings Canyon National Park to start my September trip to see the famous Rae Lakes Loop.

As we drove into the park, I couldn't believe my eyes. The Kings Canyon was magnificent with towering cliffs high above Zumwalt Meadow, which was remarkably level and stretched out for miles, it seemed. There were three or four camping areas and many RV's and tents with families enjoying themselves on their vacations. We stopped at a grocery store/restaurant where we had lunch. There was also a lodging area above the restaurant where the staff stayed for the season.

Nick and I said our goodbyes after he dropped me off at Road's End, where there was a parking lot for the hikers and backpackers.

Hiking through Zumwalt Meadow was breathtaking as I saw cliffs towering almost 2,000 ft. above the meadow. I soon came to the permit station where the Loop actually starts. After getting my permit, I walked a very level trail until I got to the junction. To my right was the Bailey Bridge and, if I'd go to my left, I would go clockwise on the Loop, which is what I decided to do. I hiked up the trail beside the South Fork of the Kings River. About two miles from the bridge I heard the roar of a waterfall. It was Mist Falls. Being that it was September, it was not as dynamic as it usually is in June or July. I stopped for a while and took pictures of the surrounding area then climbed the steep trail to Lower Paradise Valley, which had a few campsites by the river. It was the first campground that allowed overnight stay. I continued on for another mile and came upon Middle Paradise Valley, which also had a few campsites, but I decided to go another mile or so to Upper Paradise Valley. I set up camp there overnight. It was very flat and spacious. There were a few backpackers there. Lodgepoles and white firs mixed with deer brush and manzanita vegetation were the most abundant. After choosing my campsite, I pitched my tent and made myself comfortable. After an hour or so I saw a horse pack team crossing the river on an area that was less deep than where I will cross tomorrow on a log bridge. I walked over to the backpackers crossing area and it had a bridge of two downed medium sized fir trees next to each other. I will have to be very careful with my balance to make it to the other side. I

gathered some wood and made a fire in my firepit when I
noticed another camper walking towards my camp.

"Hello, there…..may I approach?" he said.

"Yes, come on up" I replied.

"I'm camping at a site about fifty yards from yours and just
wanted to say hello."

"Sure, sure, it's good to see other folks here." I said.

"My name is George." he said.

"I'm Harrison Hawk…..good to meet you, sir." I said with a smile.
He said he lived in Three Rivers and I told him about my Papo,
who also lived there. He didn't know him. He talked of some
adventures that we had experienced. I was surprised to know
that he climbed one of the Himalaya mountains with a team of
eight. I told him that I didn't trust snow and he laughed.
It would have been fun to backpack together but he was
descending and I was ascending. We hit it off pretty good and
said we might backpack together sometime in the future. We
exchanged phone numbers and said our goodbyes.

WOODS CREEK CROSSING

The next morning, I broke camp after breakfast and started on
my way to Woods Creek Crossing. I was careful walking over
those two downed trees over the river that were each about 12
inches wide. I made it across the river with no problem using my
6 ft. staff to help my balance. About 5 miles into my hike, I
looked to my left and saw the Castle Domes, a group of high
granite peaks that reminded me of the peaks that I saw in Giant

Forest that had almost the same name, Castle Rocks, which were visible from Bobcat Point in Sequoia National Park. I soon came to the popular Suspension Bridge, which crosses Woods Creek and joins the John Muir Trail. This is a very well-built bridge that extends over 100 feet or so, to my estimation. When I got to Woods Creek Crossing, I saw a young man resting on a boulder next to his backpack. I noticed a tear on the bottom of his pack as I walked up to him.

"Hi there" I yelled out.

"Howdy" he replied.

He was about my age and we chatted for a short while. I asked him about that tear in his pack. He shook his head with a smile.

"Yeah, I forgot that I had a candy bar in there and a bear ripped it and took it while I was sleeping last night."

He was on his way down towards Paradise Valley. I wished him luck and continued on my way on the John Muir Trail towards Rae Lakes.

About three and half miles on the trail, I saw a man fishing on Dollar Lake. He saw me and waved. I waved back but stayed on the trail. I stopped for a water break and he came up to me.

"How's the fishing coming along?" I asked.

"Good. I caught two but they were small and I threw them back." he answered.

He said he came over from the east side, over Baxter Pass and was fishing at Baxter Lakes yesterday. He was very friendly. His name was Ron and about middle-aged, I guessed.

"I'm doing the Loop from the west side and hope to camp at Arrowhead Lake tonight." I said.

"That's a beautiful lake. I saw a park ranger yesterday checking on visitors. She'll probably come around this afternoon again." He said.

There were dark clouds coming our way and I told him I'd better get going to find a camp. We shook hands and I left. It's great to see such friendly people up here in the High Sierra. They are lovers of nature just as I am, I thought.

RAE LAKES

When I got to Arrowhead Lake, I found a great spot to camp and pitched my tent. I looked south and saw Fin Dome up ahead, a towering monolith shooting straight upward next to the lakes. It started sprinkling and I'm glad I was prepared for it with my rain gear. I positioned my rain fly over my tent and put on my rain poncho. I decided to eat dry again so I took my nuts, jerky, and crackers out of my bag and went inside my tent. I was expecting that park ranger to come and check on me but she never came. I finished my dinner and got into my sleeping bag as the rain started coming down harder. I peeked out of my tent and saw the raindrops falling on the lake and thought about my ancestors again. I wondered if they had been here many, many years ago. I felt good but I was tired and soon fell asleep.

The next morning, I woke up to a beautiful sunrise. The rain stopped sometime during the night and there was a clean smell of pine in the air. I took a deep breath and started to get my coffee and oatmeal ready for breakfast. I was really enjoying myself. I figured that I was at my halfway point in the Loop. There were lodgepole trees and red firs along the perimeter of the lake. I knew I wanted to take a day hike to 60-Lake Basin, which is just west of where I was but to get to the trail, I had to pass the ranger station. I loaded up my gear in my backpack and started on the trail south. About two miles away, I saw the ranger station. It was a canvas tent surrounded by an electric fence, to keep the bears away. I called out to the ranger but she wasn't there. I saw a note on the fence that said she was on patrol and I figured she went south because I didn't see her on my end. I continued on and the trail crossed between two of the lakes. I saw the trail to 60-Lake Basin and I hiked up to it. I climbed up the switchbacks and saw Fin Dome to my right. When I got to the top of the ridge, I saw a small lake but kept walking on the trail. I noticed the dark clouds moving over me again and I was hoping it wouldn't start pouring down on me. When I got to a bigger lake by the trail, I saw a gold-colored tent pitched right by it and a young woman coming out of it. She was about in her 20's, I guessed and beautiful with long blond hair. I walked towards her, expecting to meet her just as a man about her age came out of their tent. I stopped and, although disappointed, I waved and forced a smile as they waved back. As I continued my walk, it started raining. I rushed under a tree for some kind of shelter, dropped my pack and took out my rain gear. The rain really started to pour so I just hunkered down and waited for it to stop. After about thirty minutes, it subsided and I continued to see the rest of the lakes. I was now on the west side of Fin Dome. I continued on the trail to see more of the lakes and then the trail just seemed to end.....a dead end. I stopped and rested for a while munching on some raisins. The skies cleared up and now it was bright and sunny. I hiked back to Rae Lakes and found a campsite near the ranger station. The ranger was still gone but I was pretty sure I would see her before I'd leave the lakes the next day. Rangers usually come to check on backpackers in the late afternoon. I waited and waited but she never came. The sunset was spectacular that evening, with yellow-gold, lavenders, and orange-red colors shining brilliantly on the granite towers of Black Mountain and Dragon Peak.

GLEN PASS

I woke up at sunrise and walked out of my tent. I saw two tents pitched near me. They were both bright blue in color but no one in sight. I figured they were still asleep. I hurried up to make my breakfast, ate, packed up my gear and left quietly, as not to disturb them. The morning sun was shining on the granite dome called Painted Lady and I couldn't believe the beauty it created on those mixed minerals of gold, orange, purples, and reds, which explained its name.

I started my ascent to Glen Pass. It was a hard climb which has an elevation of 11, 978 feet. As I hiked up the cream-colored granite, I saw several small lakes to my right. I continued on and froze in my tracks because about 100 yards away I saw a bear digging into the granite. He was in deep concentration and sticking his nose into the hole he made. I figured he could smell a rodent, possibly a Pika, those small rat-like rodents that live in high elevations underground amid the granite. I soon made it to the peak of Glen Pass and looked to the other side of the mountain where I saw a small lake by the trail. About two and a half miles from the Pass, I saw a sign that stated "Charlotte Lake 1.5 miles". I followed that trail and soon came to a ranger station.

I didn't check in and kept walking to the northwest end of the lake. There was a nice campsite about twenty feet from the lake so I decided to camp there for the night. The outlet of the lake created Charlotte Creek which, according to my map, drained into Bubbs Creek. I was tempted to follow that creek on the next morning as a short cut to finish the Loop but I decided not to. I wanted to follow the Loop as it was on the map.

BUBBS CREEK

The next morning, I broke camp early and left without eating breakfast. I was hoping to check in at the station but still there was no sign of the ranger. I didn't want to wake him or her up, since it was daybreak, so I continued to the main trail. The climb had switchbacks to the junction of Bullfrog Lake but I wanted to get to Bubbs Creek that day. After passing Vidette Meadow, the trail continued down to the Junction Meadow, where going south would lead to East Lake. I was now at the foot of Bubbs Creek and the trail was relatively straight and going down in elevation gradually. I passed the Charlotte Creek inlet and continued down to the Sphinx Creek Trail Junction.

There were campsites there and I found one that was a little higher from the trail. After pitching my tent and had a big lunch, since I skipped breakfast that morning, I saw a woman walking up to my camp. She was very short, maybe under five feet and had a ranger uniform but what was alarming was that she had a revolver in a holster balancing over her left shoulder. She was not friendly at all and kept looking for a Park Service rule that I may have broken. I wondered if she was a drill sergeant in the marines. She was checking all my supplies. I complied with all her demands and answered her questions. Since my skin was darker than her snow-white skin and my hair was long, I wondered if that was the reason for her arrogance. I thought about reporting her when I'd get back to civilization but, after thinking about it, I didn't want to start problems. I wondered if she was the Charlotte Lake ranger and if so, I'm glad I left Charlotte Lake when I did .

RATTLESNAKES

That afternoon, I walked back to the trail to fill my canteens at the creek and saw a baby rattlesnake on the edge of the trail. I couldn't believe there were rattlers in these mountains but after checking my map, we were only close to

6,000 feet in elevation. Passing through another campsite, I saw another rattlesnake....a big one. I figured there was maybe a snake den close by so I wanted to get out of there as soon as possible. As I walked back to camp, I looked at the sun and it was shining just above the monument they call the Sphinx. It was breathtaking because it really looked like the Sphinx in Egypt. It was amazing.

The next morning, I made my last breakfast of coffee, oatmeal, and added some wild strawberries that were growing nearby. I sat on a log and enjoyed my meal and marveled at the beauty of this area. After breakfast, I leaned back on a lodgepole tree and saw a horse pack train of horses and mules slowly walking up the trail. The lead packer was on his horse leading two mules with supplies and a second packer was leading two more mules as they rode up Bubbs Creek. I figured they were dropping off those supplies somewhere up the creek for other backpackers that wanted to walk without the weight. After thirty minutes or so later, there were four hikers without packs going up Bubbs. I was pretty sure they were a part of that horse pack team.

When I got back to Roads End, I had completed the Rae Lakes Loop and was proud of myself. It was a long trip and I felt strong, even though I was tired. I found a wooden table, sat down and had nuts and cranberries with my water. A Steller's Jay landed on a branch of a large lodgepole hoping I would give him a nut or two, which I did, but that was a mistake because soon half a dozen of them came down and hoped to join a potential feast. Since it was the end of my trip, I left some nuts on the table and walked back to that restaurant and call Nick to pick me up. It was a great adventure and I learned a lot. As I walked along the road, I thought I heard that raven cawing. I looked around but didn't see him. Was he really there or was it my imagination? That raven is still on my mind, ever since my first solo backpacking trip but I'm not superstitious.....or am I?

Harrison Hawk

Sequoia Mountain Man

(a book of Adventures in the Wild – episode 6)

by

Connor Corkill

COLBY PASS LOOP

DRIFTER AND BUFORD

When Nick drove up to meet me at Cedar Grove for my return trip home, I was surprised that my brother, Pablo, was with him. He had his backpack ready to hike and he brought me new supplies of food and other items. He told me he had already paid for the Cedar Grove Horse Stables to take us up to Avalanche Pass.

"It's my birthday gift to you, brother" Pablo said.

"My birthday is not until October 1$^{st.}$" I reminded him.

"Yes, but we'll be up on the mountain on that day without having to carry our heavy packs. The mules will carry them. It's the Colby Pass Loop you said you wanted to do after Rae Lakes" he said.

"Yes, that's one of the trails I wanted to do but I'm a little tired right now." I said.

"We'll relax for two nights here at a campsite before we go up. The horse packer will load the mules and we'll ride horses." he said.

I was happy to have my brother, Pablo, join me on this strenuous backpack trip that starts at Cedar Grove and makes a huge loop onto the John Muir Trail and back around to Cedar Grove. Pablo had the map ready to show me the plan.

After resting for two nights at the campground, we filled out packs with food and supplies. Nick had also stayed with us at the camp. He dropped us off at the horse stables. We thanked him and he said he'd pick us up when we call him, then he drove off.

Pablo checked in with the office and the manager introduced us to Ralph, our horse packer. He chose the horses for us to ride and loaded up one mule with both our backpacks, one on each side of the mule. My horse was named "Drifter" and Pablo's was "Buford". They were good strong horses and Ralph had already saddled them. I heard Drifter blow. Ralph grabbed the cheek of the bridle and moved him in a mounting position for me. I grabbed the safety knob of the saddle, inserted my foot in the stirrup and mounted him. Buford was a bigger, stronger horse than mine. Pablo noticed there was a tear on the cantle of the saddle, so Ralph threw a blanket over it to cushion it and Pablo mounted him.

Ralph took the lead on his horse and controlled the reins of the mule. I followed and Pablo was in the rear. We rode up Bubbs Creek to the Sphinx junction and started our climb up to Avalanche Pass. It was a very steep climb and Pablo and I had to dismount in a certain section and walk our horses up that dangerous path. I could hear the clattering the horseshoes made on the shale as we climbed. We mounted our horses when it was farther away from the edge of the cliff. Their hoofs rattled on the granite slab. Ralph led us to a small, grassy meadow and dismounted.

"This is as far as our horses are allowed to go" he said.

"But we still have to climb farther to the Pass" I complained.

"Yeah, but it's not that far….maybe a hundred yards or so and it's not that steep anymore." he said.

Pablo and I looked at each other, shrugged our shoulders with a frown and dismounted. Ralph untied and removed our packs from the mule. He connected the reins of the animals to each other and left. Pablo and I loaded the packs on our backs and started up the mountain. We soon reached the Pass and went over it. We descended about two miles and came to Moraine Meadows. We decided to camp there overnight. There was a long slab of granite next to our camp which was among lodgepoles and red firs shading our campsite. There was a creek nearby and we filled our canteens. Pablo decided to explore the area a bit as I got things ready for our dinner. He came back an hour later and said there was a makeshift shelter that some old pioneer or sheepherder must have made a hundred years ago. I didn't feel like going to see it so I just heated our dinner of pasta, biscuits, and jerky for our meal, sat on that granite slab and ate dinner.

"Tomorrow's your birthday, bro" Pablo said.

"Yeah, I know……twenty-four years." I said.

THE BEATLES

Pablo and I chatted for awhile, thinking about how we used to sing together as kids.

"That reminds me, bro….did you see those four guys singing on the Ed Sullivan show early this year?" Pablo recalled.

"Yeah, I saw them…The Beatles….they were pretty good." I said.

"They say that two of those guys wrote their songs. That's hard to believe cause those were pretty good songs….professional." Pablo said.

"Yeah, if it's true, those guys might write more hits." I said.

We also talked about the Viet Nam war and how all the protesters were marching.

We made a nice small fire and talked until after dark, since we weren't tired and didn't have a long hike that day. We sang one of the Beatles songs together.

"We don't sing as good as they do, bro, but their songs make me feel good." Pablo said.

We looked up and saw a million bright stars in heavens while humming more music. The stars seemed so close we could touch them. We soon got sleepy and went to bed.

The next morning, I peeked out of my tent and yelled out, "Whoa….". There was snow all around us. It snowed while we were sleeping. It wasn't deep, maybe two inches but it was a surprise. Pablo heard me yell and came out of his tent.

"We usually don't get the first snow until about the middle of October but here it is already." I said.

"Well, it should burn off when the sun hits it." Pablo said.

"I hope so….we have a long way to go." I said, as I looked up at the clouds.

We hiked on to Roaring River Ranger Station and by the afternoon the snow had melted off. We met the ranger, Tom, who was a man in his 20's. He was very nice and gave us good information about Cloud Canyon, which was our next destination. We decided to continue on that day instead of camping for the night, so we left.

 After about six or seven very level and easy miles, we came to a beautiful long meadow, where we saw two fishermen casting their lines on a small lake. They didn't see us so we kept on walking. We arrived at the base of the Whaleback Ridge, a long slab of pinkish-cream colored granite that resembled the back of a whale. We made camp there and thought we'd start the climb in the morning. To the west of our camp was Glacier Ridge. The next morning, we climbed the steep granite steps up toward Colby Lake, where we found a nice flat plateau to pitch our tents. We were above the lake and could see it perfectly from our camp.

COLBY PASS

At dawn the next morning, my tent was shaking really hard from a strong wind. I thought it might blow off with me in it. I looked out and noticed that the clothing line I made to dry my clothes was swinging side to side with all my clothes on the ground. I picked up the clothes in haste and, looking at the dark rain clouds, we packed our bags and found shelter under a tree near the lake. As quickly as the wind blew in, it blew out and the sun was shining.....so strange.

The rugged trail up to Colby Pass was tough with steep switchbacks near the end to the top. On the second to the last switchback, we noticed that a section of the trail was washed away. It must have been wiped out when a huge boulder rolled off the mountain and demolished it. Pablo and I had to take our packs off and toss them, one by one, over the broken section of the trail. If our packs rolled, they would have fallen down the mountain and we'd have to backtrack down and retrieve them. We then had to jump to the other side one at a time. We barely made it, since the trail was only about three feet wide. We looked at each other and crossed ourselves before jumping.

When we got on top of the Pass and looked over it, we could see Triple Divide Peak and the whole row of peaks beside it. We slowly crawled down the steep trail on our hands and knees, since it was very dangerous and slippery with granite pebbles. We didn't see any footprints at all on this trail. We eventually reached Gallats Lake, which isin't really a lake anymore. It's turning into a meadow with just a creek meandering through it. Just passed Gallats and around a bend, there was a waterfall of about 15 feet high we were tempted to camp by this beautiful spot but Pablo wanted to move on. We kept walking and hoped to get to Junction Meadow on the Kern River before dusk. We were getting tired but dragged on with the last of our energy. Pablo started singing a Mexican song to lift our spirits and it helped because it was a marching type of song that kept us going.

"You sound good, Pablo" I said with encouragement.

"Not as good as The Beatles, but it will carry us through." he said.

KERN RIVER JUNCTION MEADOW

We finally finished crossing one of the hardest legs that I've ever backpacked. I was glad that Pablo was with me or it might have been impossible. We helped each other with courage and inspiration.

Kern River Junction Meadow was a welcome site. It was a campsite with plenty of dry wood for a fire and lots of shade from all the white firs and lodgepole trees around. The great Kern River was next to us so we had a lot to be thankful for. We decided to stay there two nights in order to recover from the last few hard days that we experienced. On our layover day, two older gentlemen joined our camp area. They were from Lone Pine and said they were also brothers, Jim and Bob, and said they have been backpacking for over 40 years. I believed them because they shared their heavy supplies with each other and taught us a few things to make it easier to enjoy the hard and tough physicality that backpacking requires. We shared our stories of what we had endured the last few years and they were really nice guys. They joined our firepit and they shared some of their whisky with us during our conversations.

The next morning, we woke up to find that they were gone. They must have left real early, since it was early dawn. Last night they told us they were going over Mt. Whitney and back to Lone Pine. Anyway, Pablo and I enjoyed our coffee while we checked the map. Our plan was to continue straight up to the headwaters of the Kern River and circle around to the JMT.

Our hike started northward on the trail just east of the river. It was a gradual slight elevation climb. About a ¼ mile down, we reached the Wallace Creek junction, which would take hikers up to the JMT. We were sure that Jim and Bob went up that trail on their way to Mt. Whitney. We kept going up the river and about five miles down we had to cross it. Luckily, it was easier than I expected, being that it was now October and the first hard snowfall hasn't hit us yet. The trail started to get pretty steep. We finally got up to the first alpine lake where the wind started picking up pretty good. We were now up at about 10,700 ft. now at the start of the Upper Kern Loop Trail. We went through some forested area and then hit some brooks through alpine grasses over the granite slabs. It was like a winter wonderland but without snow, it was a very cold wind blowing about thirty miles an hour right into our faces. We managed to get to Lake South America, named because of its shape, but we didn't stay long as the wind was getting stronger and colder. The trail turned south and we were relieved because now the wind was in our backs. After a couple of miles, we hit the Kern Cutoff Junction and went east to the JMT. We were completely exhausted by then and couldn't find a place to camp. We then saw a huge boulder that was blocking the wind and we decided to just spread out our sleeping bags and spend the night there without even pitching our tents. The freezing wind kept blowing all night, it seemed, but we stayed completely inside our sleeping bags using our packs as a pillow. The sky was clear of clouds and the stars were brilliantly displayed in all their glory. We weren't concerned about a visiting bear, since we were so high in elevation that there was no food for them up here. If we did see one, it would be because they were just passing over the mountain to get to the other side.

FORESTER PASS

We woke up when the sun hit us in the morning. The wind had subsided but it was still cold. I got out of my sleeping bag and woke Pablo up.
"Hey, Pablo……how are you doing, buddy." I said, as I shook his bag.
"Are we home yet?" he answered.
"I'm glad you still have a sense of humor" I said.

He smiled and slowly got out of his bag. We looked at the magnificent alpine area that we were in the middle of. We really needed some hot coffee to warm us up but I was getting low on propane. Pablo had some so we used his fuel to heat up some water from our canteens. After coffee and granola, we packed up and started towards Forester Pass.

As we dragged our legs on that hard granite, we marveled at the Diamond Mesa to our right. It was about four miles to the Pass and we knew that it was the highest Pass on the JMT at 13,180 feet. We finally got to the top after traversing over many switchbacks and now we were on the Kings Kern Divide. We looked north and saw the lakes and more alpine to cross before we could find a campsite in a forested area. We wanted to camp at Center Basin but when we got there, we noticed that the trail was obscured by vegetation. I remembered that a ranger told me the trail to Golden Bear Lake was discouraged to hikers ever since a couple of fatalities happened there, so we found a campsite by the river. We were finally out of the alpine granite and in forested land, to our delight. This was our next to last campsite and it was a beautiful grassy area with sunshine warming out tired bodies. We slept very well that night inside our tents and I was anxious to finish our trip, since I had just finished the Rae Lakes Loop just before this one. I was ready for some hot pizza and a cold beer.

BUBBS CREEK

The next day, we hiked on Bubbs Creek down to Vidette Meadow. The Kearsarge Pinnacles, to our right, were amazing granite towers that stood high on that granite ridge. We left the JMT when we got to the junction where the Glen Pass and Bubbs Creek meet. We decided to camp where Charlotte Creek meets Bubbs Creek. We were getting low on food and fuel by that time so we heated the last of our dinners but saved some fuel for our morning coffee.

We were lucky to finish our trip without any injuries, after what we went through. We had enough to eat and were warm enough to survive. Pablo and I talked about our ancestors and wondered how they could have survived if they went through what we went through. It was much harder in those days. We talked about how proud we were of the blood we shared with each other and our ancestors. We left Charlotte Creek camp back to Roads End and called Nick to pick us up. I thought about this last trip. It was the hardest one I've had so far and there will be harder ones ahead. I won't have Pablo with me for each one so I'll have to get tougher and stronger as time goes on.

Harrison Hawk

Sequoia Mountain Man

(a book of Adventures in the Wild – episode 7)

by

Connor Corkill

MINERAL KING

TIMBER GAP

It was a long and winding road from Highway 198 to Mineral King. The twenty-five miles had over 600 turns. Nick and I had never been to Mineral King so we planned to camp at Cold Springs Campground for two nights so I could get acclimated before my backpack trip, since I'll be starting at 7,500 feet elevation.

In the 1870's, prospectors hoped to strike it rich in the Mineral King Valley with the silver ore that was found in this area but they found out that it was too hard and costly to transfer the ore out of the area to the mills. What was interesting to me was that there was evidence that Indians were present here 1,000 years ago because there were bedrock mortars and food-grinding holes worn deep into solid rock. Perhaps some of my ancestors came here around that time.

Nick and I chose a nice campsite at Cold Springs Campground, near the East Fork of the Kaweah River. It had a bear box and trees with plenty of shade. I really liked this campsite and we each pitched our own tent. There was a faucet with drinking water and was worth every penny of the camping fee. I was well acclimated there for two nights and Nick decided to stay in that spot for two weeks so he won't have to come back to pick me up after my hike is over. So, the morning of my first leg we had a big breakfast of eggs, bacon, and biscuits that we cooked over the grill that was furnished by the camp. We had a very sturdy table to eat on and after that, I was ready to start my hike over Timber Gap.

Nick drove me the one mile to the trailhead and wished me luck.

"I'll be waiting for you at this same campsite, my friend." he said.

"Thank you, Nick, I plan to be back before those two weeks are over." I said.

Nick and I became good friends and he knew that my quest for adventure was strong and that I wanted to see and feel what my ancestors felt centuries ago.

I started up the trailhead with sage being the prominent vegetation along the Monarch Trail. The trail would branch out to different paths, one going to Monarch Lake, another one to Cobalt and Crystal Lake. I stayed left and passed through a red fir forest until I came to an open slope. Since we were in early August, there were flowers blooming including Indian paintbrush and blue bells.

There was a family of marmots that were present near the larger granite boulders that were protruding from the grassy field. They kept their eye on me and retreated into their dens when I got too close. I continued on a straight, slight elevation gain until I reached a large timber stand called Timber Gap. I thought that there was no creek, no water. I looked over the edge on the north side of the Gap and there were switchbacks going down for a long way.

CLIFF CREEK

It was a long 3.5-mile descent to Cliff Creek. The trail had a beautiful and ever-changing terrain of red firs, a field of ferns, granite rock slabs, a deep gully to my left, and a large variety of colorful flowers along the way.

When I got to the creek, I found a large snag that had fallen over the length of the creek so I was able to carefully walk over it to get to the other side and onto the camp area. Cliff Creek was a very dense, forested area that only had about 3 campsites. What I didn't like about this camp was that it was so dense in vegetation and trees, that there could be a bear hiding behind a tree only ten feet away and I wouldn't know it. So, I had to be very careful with my food, since there was no bear box around. I found a good, high branch of about fifteen feet high where I could hang my food. After securing my edibles, I pitched my tent and unpacked my bag and went to the creek to rinse off my dust and dirt. There was a twelve-feet high waterfall near the camp and a small sandy area where I could kneel and filter my water into my canteens. I took my clothes off and rinsed my body, dried off, put on some dry, clean clothes, then rinsed my dirty clothes in the creek. This is my regular routine after every leg that I take backpacking. I like feeling clean before I get in my sleeping bag for the night. I stretched out a thin, camo nylon rope from one tree to another and hung my wet clothes. They will dry overnight. I found some dry wood and made a small fire to keep me warm, since the sun doesn't shine in a dense area like this. I was tired and didn't feel like cooking so I ate some nuts and dried fruit with water. It started to get pretty dark and, after looking at my watch, it wasn't even sunset yet. It was cold but I was warm in my dry clothes with a good, hot fire next to me. I started hearing branches moving and then saw three hikers going down the trail at a quick pace. I waved at them, hoping to have a chat, but they seemed to be in a real hurry, as one of them waved back but kept their fast pace. Some hikers like to brag about how fast they can hike by going from point A to point B. I like to stop and 'smell the roses' by just soaking in all the beauty from time to time.

When it got pretty dark, I put out the fire and went in my tent. I turned on my headlamp and checked my map for awhile until I heard some twigs snap. I reached for my flashlight. I couldn't tell which way the sounds were coming from but I thought it was either a person or a bear. I didn't hear any more twig-snapping so I eventually fell asleep but kept waking up through the night when I thought I heard sounds.

Right before dawn, I got up and started the fire again by adding kindling to some of the hot coals that were under the ashes. I added some twigs and soon had a warm fire. I retrieved my food that was hanging from the branch and wrapped up my line. I wanted to heat my water, drink my coffee, eat a granola bar and leave as soon as possible. I didn't see any bear tracks around my camp to I felt at ease about that. After breakfast, I packed up all my gear into my pack and walked up the trail towards Pinto Lake.

PINTO LAKE

About four miles up the trail, I stopped for a water break and found a boulder I could sit on that was about twenty feet from the trail. As I was drinking and enjoying the scenery, I saw a big man hiking in the same direction that I was planning to go to. He looked like a tall, muscular fellow but what was interesting to see is that he was holding a very small, white umbrella over his head to shade himself from the sun. I closed my eyes and shook my head, then opened them wide to make sure I wasn't hallucinating. He was real alright. He didn't see me and I didn't want to start a conversation, in case the muscle man might not like me making fun of his little umbrella. I let him pass ahead of me and thought I might see him at Pinto.

The trail started getting a little steeper and there were no trees, so the hot sun was bearing down on me. When I got to Pinto Lake, I noticed that it wasn't a lake anymore. It was just a creek meandering through a meadow. I read in my books in college that over thousands of years, a small lake eventually changes into a meadow, and a meadow eventually changes into a forest.

The first thing I saw at Pinto Lake was a bear box. I opened the latch and noticed it was empty. I put my food in it and looked for a good campsite. I found a flat area under some lodgepoles that was perfect. I pitched my tent and spread my supplies in and around it. It was a nice camp with plenty of lodgepoles amid the granite slabs. There were red firs and some manzanita brush growing in the area. I walked around to explore the place a bit and found a round, metal plate with a handle on it on the ground. I wasn't sure what it was. I wondered if it was an old miner's storage container or maybe a surveyor's mark of some kind. Anyway, I opened it, looked inside and it was an empty cylinder about two feet into the ground. It was encased with metal and I realized it was a bear-proof container that must have been used many, many years ago. I closed it up and went back to camp.

As I was sorting through my supplies, I heard some people talking and laughing. I looked toward the bear box and saw two oriental guys opening the bear box and putting their food in it. They were in a good mood, it looked like, but I just watched them as they then looked around for a camp site. They saw me and waved with big smiles on their faces. I was glad to see that. I was wondering if the big muscular fellow with the umbrella was around too but I didn't see him.

I went to pick up my food from the bear box to make my dinner and was surprised to see a quart of an unopened glass bottle of Jack Daniels whisky. I can't couldn't believe they brought something that heavy. I took my food out and walked back to my camp. After cooking my pasta and eating it, the two guys walked to my camp. They introduced themselves but I couldn't understand them with their strong accents to make out their names, so I just remembered them as 'the short guy' and 'the tall guy'. They said they were students at Stanford University and were going to Little 5 Lakes tomorrow. I told them that I was too. We chatted for awhile and I could understand most of what they were saying, even with their strong accent.

"Have you seen a big fellow near your camp?" I asked.

"No, no one else is here except you and us." the short guy said. I told them about the child's umbrella that he had over his head and they laughed, but then the tall guy said that he probably had a child's umbrella so he wouldn't have to carry the weight of an adults larger and heavier one. I agreed but I wondered why they didn't think twice about carrying the weight of that heavy quart glass bottle of Jack Daniels whisky.

Back at my camp, I was getting ready to turn in when I saw eight bucks that came close to my area. There were three six-pointers and five younger bucks following them. The big bucks were sniffing around while the younger ones were clashing their antlers with each other in a non-threatening display of dominance. I really enjoyed watching them until the big bucks decided to move on and the younger ones followed.

The next morning, I woke up early and noticed that the two guys were gone. I went to the bear box and they had taken their food and the bottle. After eating a breakfast of coffee and oatmeal, I packed my gear and started my hike up to Black Rock Pass in that cold and foggy morning.

BLACK ROCK PASS

Climbing up the trail, I could not see the Pass because the low clouds, or fog, were obscuring it but I could see Spring Lake to my right and I knew that Mineral King was on the other side of it, according to my map. The higher I climbed, the wetter the clouds seemed to get. I was getting soaked with moisture and it was cold. Before long, the clouds were so thick around me that I could only see about five feet ahead of me, so I just concentrated on making sure I'd keep my eyes on the trail or I might stray away from it. My legs just dragged on until I finally made it to the top. The pack on my back felt heavier than usual but I think it was because it was wet and my clothes were soaked with the moisture and made them heavy. At the Pass, I was surprised to see the two oriental guys sitting on a boulder with the bottle of Jack Daniels in the short guy's hand. They saw me and welcomed me.

"Hey, Harrison, you made it." he said with slurred speech.

"Yes, I made it but it was cold and very damp coming up." I said.

I could tell they had already opened the bottle and were drinking some of it.

"Here.....have a swig of our Jack Daniels." The short guy said as he handed me the bottle.

I grabbed it and, noticing that it was half empty, I told them it was too early in the day for me but I thanked them anyway. I handed the bottle back to him and thought it was a bad idea to drink that much alcohol at this elevation, even if shared by two people.

"We saved this bottle to take pictures up here with it and show our friends back at the University." the tall guy said.

"Well, just be careful because you still have more hiking to do." I warned them.

"Yeah, but it's all downhill from here to Little 5 Lakes so we'll be ok." the short guy said.

"I'm going to head on down. I'm all wet and cold." I said.

"We're wet too but we don't mind because Jack is our friend." he said as they both laughed.

"I'll see you guys down at camp. Be careful and I wouldn't drink anymore of Jack. It can be dangerous. The alcohol will have more of an effect on you at a high elevation." I warned.

"OK, see you down there later, my friend." the tall guy said.

I waved and started down the mountain.

I finally got to the bottom of the granite trail and crossed small streams until I got to Little 5 Lakes and a row of bear boxes. I saw a canvas tent to my right and I knew that it was the ranger station but I wanted to put my food away and find a campsite first, before I go to meet the ranger. I walked around the campground and saw about six or seven gold-colored tents all in a row, so I figured they were together….possibly a church group or a club of some kind, I thought.

LITTLE FIVE LAKES

I saw a man sitting on a folding chair in front of one of the tents. I walked up to him and introduced myself. He said his name was "Tom" and that he was an assistant to the main Boy Scout Leader and all the tents were for boy scouts.
"There are two guys up at Black Rock Pass that will be coming down soon." I said.
"Are they in your group?" he asked.
"No, they are students at Stanford but I'd like to talk to the ranger about them. They may need some help coming down." I said.
I told him about the Jack Daniels and that they were drinking at the Pass.
"Well, the ranger is on patrol right now so I'm not sure when she might come back." he said.
"Ok, well, I'm going to find a campsite and get settled in…..talk to you later." I said.
"Ok, if I see her before you do, I'll tell her about those guys….thanks." he said.

I looked around to find a campsite away from the boy scouts, since I know those boys will be loud and talkative. I found one about forty yards away and set up my tent and gear. I went to the four bear boxes to put my food away. I opened all of the boxes and they were all full so I squeezed my food in a corner of one of them and locked it up.

I walked to the large canvas tent that was up on a slope of a hill. There was a metal fence around it with a sign that said, "Warning, electric fence". I made sure I didn't touch it but walked around to see what supplies she had outside. I saw a large crate, which probably had tools in it. There was a shovel, an axe with firewood nearby, and some folded up tarps.

In the late afternoon, I started hearing lots of voices getting louder and louder. I knew that it was the group of boy scouts coming back from a day hike. I didn't want to bother them on my first day here. I was tired and just wanted to take it easy. I kept thinking about the two guys on top of the Pass, since I still hadn't seen them come down. There were some dark clouds rolling in and thought it might start raining soon. I started to hear thunder and, as I expected, it soon started sprinkling. I looked up towards the Pass and thought those two guys might come down drenched with rain water and stumbling on the trail, if they drank that whole bottle of alcohol. I know that college students love to party and drink but up here it is too dangerous. I then heard a loud thunder clap and it started pouring rain. I got inside my tent and thought about those two drunken fools up on the mountain.

The next morning, the sun was shining and there were puddles of water all over the place. I looked up at the Pass to see what was visible. It was clear but I didn't see anything or anyone. I walked to the ranger station to tell her about the two guys that might still be up there.

"Hello…..anyone there?" I yelled out.

The ranger walked out to meet me.

"Hi there, are you with the boy scouts crew?" she asked.

"No, I'm Harrison Hawk and last night I was hoping to see you because there were two guys up at the Pass that might need your help." I blurted out.

Just as I finished that statement, 'the short guy' walks out of her tent.

"Harrison, how are you doing, buddy?" he said with a cup of coffee in his hand.

"Oh, man, I thought you guys were in trouble." I said with obvious relief.

They both laughed and 'the tall guy' walked out of the tent and joined the laughter.

"No, we're fine. We got wet but made it back down here with thunder and lightning all around us." the short guy said.

The ranger smiled and said she was coming from Pinto Lake, saw them as they were hiking down and helped them.

"Well, that's a relief. I was worried about you guys." I said.

"Thank you for thinking of us, Harrison. Everything is fine now." the tall guy said.

I walked back to my tent and finally started to have my first cup of coffee and a nice hot breakfast. I thought about day hiking to see the lakes around the area but it was too wet and muddy in some place, so I just got lazy and relaxed with the sounds of boy scouts shouting and laughing at a distance.

BIG FIVE LAKES

The next day, I knew I would be having a bit of trouble crossing creeks and possible inlets or outlets of lakes because of the hard rain we had yesterday. The sky was clear and sunny so it might be ok if I'm careful. It was only two miles to the junction of seeing the biggest of the Big Five Lakes, according to my map. It was a pretty easy trail and I was soon at the junction. I wanted to see the biggest lake so I went to my right and noticed that there was nothing except horseshoe prints on the ground. There weren't any boot prints, so it must not be very popular with hikers on foot, I thought.
I walked about a mile and saw the biggest lake of the five. I noticed that the reason it's not too popular with campers was because there weren't any good campsites, so I left back to the junction and went down to the lower lake. It was a beautiful lake with many campsites near the water and I chose one up on a hill. I stayed there two nights, since it was so beautiful. I didn't see any other campers while I was there. When it was time to go, I had to cross a log jam on the outlet of the lake. It was a bit scary because I had to choose which logs were secure enough for me to stay upright but my staff helped me get across with no problem.

SAWTOOTH PASS

I crossed the short bridge and walked the almost four miles of Lost Canyon to Columbine Lake, which is on the east side of Sawtooth Pass and which is part of the Great Western Divide.

I wanted to climb up to Sawtooth Peak, which is 12,343 feet but from the Pass, I would have to climb about another 800 feet over large boulders and it was pretty hard to do. I decided to go over Sawtooth Pass and at the top, I could see Mineral King Valley and to the end of my loop. When I started down, the ground was nothing but granite pebbles and small rocks where my boot just started sinking halfway down into it. I had to walk adjacent to the trail in order to get more of a solid grip on the trail. The reason it was so loose was because it's been so overused that it just breaks down into granules so it makes hikers sink into the trail.

I finally got down to Moraine Lake, which has very large camping area just below the lake. I was tempted to camp there among the marmots and other little creatures but I decided to go down to the Valley and call it a good, nice loop. I was also thinking about seeing Nick, who had some real food and maybe a beer or two for me. This was a great experience that I'll never forget. I also know that there are many other trails here in Mineral King that I want to experience and will do that soon.

Harrison Hawk

Sequoia Mountain Man

(a book of Adventures in the Wild – episode 8)

by

Connor Corkill

DAY HIKING MINERAL KING

As I entered into Mineral King Valley, I knew that Nick would be waiting for me at a campsite. When I got down from Monarch Trail, I still had to walk another mile to Cold Springs Campground. When I got to the campsite, I was surprised to see Pablo's 'Caballo' motorcycle parked there.

"Here he comes" Pablo said as he walked towards me.

 "Pablo, when did you get here, bro?" I said.

"I got here yesterday afternoon. I knew you and Nick were here" he answered

"How was your trip, Harry?" Nick said.

"It was great…..good experiences." I said.

"Well, Pablo would like to day hike to a few places, since I have already paid for four more nights here" Nick said.

"I'd like to rest before I go anywhere" I said.

"Sure, sure, we understand…..take it easy for a couple of hours" Pablo said.

 We all laughed and Pablo handed me a beer from the ice chest.

I told them about the two oriental guys and the bottle of Jack Daniels.

"Well, I only brought some beer, bro" Pablo said.

"Yeah, good, I don't like whisky anyway" I said.

They laughed when I told them about the muscleman and his little umbrella. It was good to be back at camp with my brother and my friend. Nick took out three steaks from the ice chest and three large potatoes from his food cache.

"We're going to have a good meal tonight." Nick said.

	After dinner, we sat around the fire and drank Sierra Nevada beer, our favorite. I told them about my experiences on my last hike and the expectations I had in hoping to find evidence of our ancestors in the area but nothing was found.

I added more wood to the fire and we talked by the fire until midnight. We checked the map and decided to go to the five Mosquito Lakes the next morning, to Eagle Lake the next day, and to White Chief Lake on our last day on camping, since, we only have four more nights here at Cold Springs Campground.

MOSQUITO LAKES

I woke up to the smell of coffee in the morning. I peeked out of my tent to see Nick, making breakfast of eggs, bacon, and biscuits. Pablo was still asleep. I got up and poured a cup of coffee from the percolator.

"Did you sleep well?" Nick asked.

"Yes, and had a strange dream." I answered.

"I dreamt that there was a giant talking marmot that was telling me to go home." I said.

We both laughed and our laughter woke Pablo up.

"What's so funny" Pablo said.

I told him about my dream and how the animals of the mountains didn't want us there. And they could all talk and complained about mankind destroying their environment.

"Well, that's true, to a certain extent" Nick said.

"Yes, but I believe in the mission of the Park Service. They are protecting the most fragile and environmentally challenged areas of our country." I said.

"I could have been a park ranger because I have a degree in Outdoor Recreation and I might do it someday but decided that I wanted more freedom to explore the beauty that our ancestors saw and felt before I make a decision about that." I said.

We packed our bags for a day hike to Mosquito Lakes and left around ten that morning. We decided to hike through the Cold Springs Nature Trail on our way to the Mosquito Lakes trailhead. It was a very level trail that runs parallel to the East Fork of the Kaweah River. The flowers were blooming throughout the trail with Indian Paintbrush, Leopard Lilly and other colorful species. We arrived at the parking lot, where other hikers park their cars before going up. This trailhead, according to the map, is the same trail to Eagle and White Chief for about a mile and them it splits up. After getting to that junction, we turned right to Mosquito Lakes and Eagle Lakes trails. We climbed for almost a mile to another junction that splits Eagle and Mosquito lakes. An amazing sight was seeing a giant sinkhole near that junction. It was big enough to swallow a city bus, I thought.

"That's where your giant marmot lives, Harry" Pablo said.

We all laughed.

"Yes, I can hear him talking to his other marmot friends.....getting ready to chase us out." Nick said as everyone laughed even harder.

We climbed for a quarter mile and then the trail straightened out. It made a sharp turn to the left as we swung around Miner's Nose then the trail descended to the first Mosquito Lake. It was a beautiful lake but it had a sign that said "No Camping – restoration area". I can see why they don't want any more camping there. The soil on the edge of the lake was eroding from overuse. We circled around the lake and started climbing to the second lake. It was a steep climb and we almost passed it until Nick noticed it to our right. It was a small lake. We didn't spend too much time there because we wanted to see the bigger lakes up ahead. The third lake was absolutely gorgeous with three islands in it. Pablo was so excited that he took his clothes off, except for his underwear, and jumped in the lake.

"Hey, Pablo, watch out for the giant fish that might bite you. He's got his orders from the giant marmot." Nick said as he laughed out loud.

"Don't try to scare me. It won't work." Pablo said as he quickly got out of the lake.

"I was thinking of swimming to the island in the middle of the lake but it looks too far away." Pablo said.

"No, don't try it unless you want to be food for the giant fish." Nick said laughing.
Pablo put his clothes on and we started the climb to the fourth lake. It was a very steep climb and, looking at the map, there were actually six lakes but I guess one of them was just a pond so we continued on up to the next lake. It was big and good for camping overnight, we thought. We took a break and ate our lunch of tuna sandwiches and an apple for dessert. The sun was shining and there were no trees for us to shade ourselves. Pablo

and Nick were pretty tired. They were not used to climbing at this elevation, so we turned around and hiked back to camp. We decided to just see the fifth and last lake from Miner's Ridge when we go to Eagle Lake tomorrow.

We got back to camp with about three hours left till dusk. We resumed our chores for the afternoon and Nick made some tacos with a side of beans for dinner. He also had a bag of corn chips and a bowl of store-bought potato salad. We had another great dinner, thanks to Nick. We made another fire and talked of what we experienced that day and we were ready to see an alpine lake the next day called Eagle Lake.

"I hope you don't have any more dreams of giant animals, Harry..." Nick said.

"....or giant fish" Pablo added.

We went to bed early and I fell asleep to the sound of the fast-flowing river close by. I thought about how lucky the owners of the cabins must be by inheriting them from their ancestors for summer vacations.

EAGLE LAKE

The next morning, we got an early start after breakfast and started on the Cold Springs Nature Trail, since it was closer and safer than walking on the road. There were about 5 vehicles and another one had a huge blue tarp covering the bottom section of their car. The driver of the tarped vehicle was getting ready to go on a hike. I asked him what the reason was for the wrapping.

"It's to keep the marmots out of our water and antifreeze hoses. They chew on the hoses, then the antifreeze leaks out onto the ground. When we come back from our hike or overnight trip, we start driving out and our radiator is out of water so our engine heats up." he said.

Nick and I looked at each other and we both raised our eyebrows because Nick's car wasn't wrapped. The driver said we were safe at the campground so we were relieved and continued on our way.

When we hiked up to the White Chief and Eagle junction, we turned right and went up towards the Eagle and Mosquito Lakes junction. We passed the 'giant marmot' sinkhole, as Nick called it, and climbed the 1.7 miles to Eagle Lake. It was a beautiful lake with red firs on the west side where there were camping sites and the east side which was bright, white granite and was not accessible by foot. There was a great view of Eagle Crest mountain to the southeast of the lake. We saw one man that was fishing on the southern section of the lake with two young boys sitting nearby. We climbed up the hill on the west side and found a nice shady campsite. We knew we weren't going to stay the night but we brought snacks and drinking water. There was a cool breeze blowing from the south. It was already about noon and Nick, our chef and food preparer, opened his day pack and pulled out dried cherries, cashews, and an apple for each of us. We had a nice lunch then we decided to walk up a little higher to the top of Miner's Ridge. When we got to the top, we could see the southernmost Mosquito Lake that we missed the day before. It was stretched out from the north to south and I heard that some hikers hike down to it from where we were standing but the big boulders looked like it would be a real challenge. We stayed up on the ridge for a half-hour or so then went back down. I pointed to Eagle Crest Peak. "Just on the other side of that peak should be White Chief Lake but according to the map it would have to be a cross country hike to see it." I stated.

"We'll be on the White Chief Trail tomorrow. We can decide then if we'll have enough energy to do that." Pablo said.

"I think we should stay on the trail. The map shows that it's a hard climb to get there." Nick said.

We said goodbye to Eagle Lake and went back to camp. I didn't see any evidence of my ancestors being up here, although I was pretty sure that they did. I usually look for food-grinding holes in the granite rock or mortars. It was still a great short alpine lake that is easy to see so close from our camp.

When we got back to camp, Nick was already getting our dinner ready.

"Tonight, we're having spaghetti with meat sauce and sourdough bread." he said.

"Wow, Nick, we should have you on our car-camping trips all the time. You feed us great food." I said.

"We need lots of protein and carbohydrates for our last hike tomorrow. It will be the longest and hardest, according to the map." Nick said.

We ate and went to sleep early because, yes, it will be a tough one tomorrow.

WHITE CHIEF TRAIL

We woke up at daybreak and had coffee and a big breakfast of eggs, ham, hash brown potatoes and biscuits. We all drank plenty of coffee. The caffeine will help us to get going and it sure did. We hit the trail and got to the trailhead just as the sun was coming up over Mineral Peak. The first mile to the junction was pretty easy but then it started climbing. When we climbed another mile, we made a sharp right turn and went up to the Crabtree Cabin Ruins. There wasn't much left of what was built a century ago. Old prospectors lived and worked here trying their luck at mining silver ore out of solid granite. As the trail turned left and we climbed a hill, we came across a big open field, which was about 300 feet long. There were very large snags positioned about thirty years or so from each other. It was almost like a natural "Stonehenge" in Sequoia National Park.....a large timber cemetery. It was uncanny. We walked among the giants and couldn't believe how they got there.
"They must have been washed up here on a super flood centuries ago because these timbers are petrified." I said.
"Yes, this is unreal. Maybe space aliens placed them in here." Nick said.
Pablo walked away from us, got down on his knees and started to say prayers in another language as he raised his arms to the sky. Nick and I just watched him in silence. We didn't want to bother him because it seemed this may be a religious site to him. Pablo prayed for about ten minutes then got up.
"I believe our ancestors were here and prayed here, brother." Pablo said.
"I wish there was some evidence of that, bro." I said.

"You have to feel the energy from the spirits and then you will know." Pablo said.

We continued up a quarter mile more and over a hill, we came to the top of the White Chief Basin. It looked like a huge amphitheater of granite. We walked down to the bottom where there was a small lake. It wasn't the White Chief Lake that was on the map and higher in elevation, but it was the end of the trail. There were no trees at all. We looked west and we could see White Chief Peak at 11,000 feet high. We didn't want to stay at the basin too long because the sun was getting terribly hot and we had no shade of any kind so we left. This trail was a 'in and out' one-way hiking trail so we will be seeing everything that we saw all over again. This was a great experience to see and I'm glad my brother and my good friend were with me.

We made it back to camp late afternoon and we were pretty tired. This was our last night here in this gorgeous, amazing valley called Mineral King and there were still more trails that I hadn't seen yet. I will come back and make sure I see them all, but for now, I will give thanks to God for keeping us safe and I will continue to backpack the great Sequoia National Park and Sequoia National Forest to walk the trails of my ancestors.

Harrison Hawk

Sequoia Mountain Man

(a book of Adventures in the Wild – episode 9)

by

Connor Corkill

GRANITE BASIN

COPPER CREEK TRAIL

It is now 1966 and I was planning to backpack Franklin Pass in Mineral King like I had the year before until I got an unexpected call from George, the backpacker that I met two years ago at Upper Paradise Valley during my Rae Lakes Loop trip. He invited me to accompany him to backpack Granite Basin and make a loop back through Kennedy Pass. He said we could go in his car. He lived in 3 Rivers so he picked me up and we drove to Kings Canyon National Park. It was an unusually hot day and the weather forecast was thunderstorms in the area that we were going to. We both had been in thunderstorms in the mountains and what's great about the Sierra Nevada Mountains is that they come and go quickly in an hour or two.

George drove past Hume Lake and Indian Basin. The drive down to Yucca Point was long and we finally crossed the bridge and drove alongside the South Fork of the Kings River, a beautiful and fast-moving river with rapids intensified by large boulders in the middle of the river. We stopped at Cedar Grove and had a late lunch at the restaurant that is only open in the summer. We noticed a little bit of smoke high above us and hoped it was just a small lightning fire that the firefighters would contain easily. We drove on to Road's End where we parked and started our hike on Copper Creek Trail, which climbs all the way to Granite Basin.

"Are you ready to see some beautiful country, Harrison?" George said.

"I sure am, George, I've never been to that area before." I said.

"Let's get started. We're getting a late start and I hope to get to Lower Tent Meadows before dark." he said.

We started going up from about 5,000 feet and climbed up many short switchbacks. We stopped for a water break at around 6,400 feet and, after looking at the map, still had to climb to 7,800 feet elevation to our first camp at Lower Tent Meadow. When I got up to put my pack back on, I heard the rattle of a rattlesnake. I froze. I didn't know where the rattler was but George did. He took his hiking stick and scooped up the rattler from the middle of its body and tossed it downslope into the sage brush area.

"I didn't know there were rattlers up this high." I said.

"Oh, yes, in fact there's a snake den at Bubbs and Sphinx camp."
George said.

"I believe it because I saw two rattlers on that trail when I came
back from the Rae Lakes Loop" I said.

When we got to Lower Tent Meadow, we were pretty tired and
the campsites were very small and not very appealing. We
pitched our tents, ate nuts, dried fruit and water and got in our
tents to sleep. I kept my food inside my tent and hoped that a
bear would not bother me that night. I also made sure a rattler
could not get into my tent by checking all points of entry and
checked for tent rips too.

The next morning, we got up at the break of dawn, ate a
quick breakfast and continued our climb. After climbing another
2,300 feet, we finally made it to Granite Basin. It was a flat
grassy plateau with granite boulders of different sizes spread
out on the landscape of Granite Meadow. It was smoky
throughout the area and we assumed it was coming from the
north but weren't sure if it was just clouds, smog, or fire smoke.

"I just hope it's not smoke from a fire because I've had
respiration problems in the past" George said.

"We can turn back, if you want" I said.

"No, no, let's just keep an eye on it and see if it gets worse." he
said.

"I'd like for us to go over Kennedy Pass and finish this loop."
George continued.

"OK" I said.

We walked towards Granite Lake alongside flowers blooming in
and around that beautiful Granite Meadow.

GRANITE LAKE

We continued on the trail hoping to find a campsite on Granite Lake. When we turned left at the junction, we were amazed to see a large family gathering beside a huge granite boulder. There must have been maybe two or three families camping together with lots of supplies, including tables, stoves, food canisters, ice chests, and food….the comforts of home. We also saw children that looked about 7 or 8 years old, with their parents and maybe even grandparents. We greeted them and walked up to say hello.

"Howdy, there" George yelled out.

"Hello, backpackers" a middle-aged man said with a smile.

"Well, you folks look like you carried a lot of heavy supplies on your backs" George joked.

They all laughed.

"Yes, we've got lawn chairs and beds inside our large tents. It's great. We had them brought up by mules and we rode horses up here." the man said.

"Fantastic" George said.

"My friend and I are looking for a campsite near the lake." George added.

"After exploring a bit, I saw a couple around the bend there and near the lake that I think you might like." the man said.

"Thank you" I said.

We waved to them as we walked in the direction he pointed to. They all seemed to be very nice, waving back as they smiled.

Walking to the area that the man suggested, we found a very nice campsite on a hill about thirty yards away from the lake and out of sight from the family group.

We filled our canteens at the outlet of the lake. We got settled in, pitching our tents and, after putting our bathing suits on, jumped into the lake for a refreshing rinse to wash off our dirt from the hike. It was cold but invigorating. We went back to our campsite after getting dressed and started our dinner. I could tell George was very experienced in the way he organized his supplies and prepared his food.

FOREST FIRE

In the morning, as we were walking out, the man in the family group invited George and me to have a plate of bacon, eggs, toast, and potatoes. We were so surprised and we surely welcomed it. We chatted with them as we ate breakfast, thanked them, and then continued on our way to Granite Pass, which was only a climb of about three hundred feet. When we got to the top of the Pass, we descended about 400 feet and came to the junction, which, if we turned west, would take us towards Dead Pine Ridge. We passed by some gorgeous little lakes along the way, which were part of the Volcano Lakes on the south side of the trail. We continued on towards the Ridge and started seeing more smoke but the wind was to our backs so the smoke was moving away from us. As we hiked into the forest, we started smelling the smoke and hoped it wouldn't get worse. We were getting concerned and hoped that the wind would continue to blow the smoke away from us.

"What do you think, George?" I asked
"Let's see if we can get past this Ridge and then see what it looks like." he said.
We continued on cautiously but then as we turned a corner, we saw a stand of trees completely engulfed in flames which were shooting up about ten feet high. We froze and realized that we didn't make the right choice. I couldn't smell the smoke earlier because the wind was blowing on our backs and into the fire wall. We knew we had to go back on the trail. There were now flames on our right, the north side, and I looked at George and he was in a state of panic.
"George, are you ok?" I asked.
He couldn't talk because the wind shifted and it was now swhirling the smoke around us and it was affecting George in a bad way. I started to help him because he was starting to get incoherent and in a panic. I started seeing embers hitting the trail, which were coming from exploding pinecones as the flames engulfed the trees around us. We walked faster and faster and we could hear the roar of the fire as I wrapped my arm around his and helped him out. We finally got out of the Ridge and into the granite area of the Volcano Lakes. We stopped by a flat granite slab to catch our breath. I noticed that George's hair was singed with the embers that were flying around us. I touched my hair and it was also singed by the fire. I felt we were lucky to get out. If we had gone in a little earlier, we might not have been able to get out. Just then, we saw four firefighters running out of the Ridge too. They were wearing Nomex fireproof clothing but they were very frightened too. They stopped next to us.

"Are you guys ok?" one of them asked.

"Yes,......my friend is having breathing problems but I think he'll be ok" I said.

"We can help him out." another firefighter said.

"Well, let's see how bad he is feeling." I said.

I looked at George and asked him if he wanted to go with the firefighters. He nodded his head, so I held his hand and squeezed it. I let him go and saw him walk away with them as he was coughing over and over again.

"Just take him to the next lake and I'll be there in a while." I said

"OK" one of the firefighters said.

I was overcome by the smoke myself. Why didn't I go with them too, I thought. I stayed lying on the granite for another 20 minutes trying to catch my breath. I got up and walked to the next lake to meet with George but he was gone. I was confused and just decided to stay near the lake and look for George. I realized that the firefighters took him off the mountain. It looks like I'm alone now with no ride home. At dusk, I didn't bother to pitch my tent. I just pulled out my sleeping bag and slipped in and tried to get some sleep, since I knew I'd be safe by the lake.

The next morning, I looked towards the Ridge forest and there was still smoke high above it. I could smell it and I knew I had to retreat and go back the way we came. When I got to the junction, I was going to go south and back to Granite Pass but I still had enough food for three more nights so I looked at my map and decided to go north away from the fire and see State Lakes. I passed by The Lake of The Fallen Moon, which sounded like a name that an Indian tribe would call it. I was tempted to climb up and see it but maybe on the way back, I thought. I continued walking north through an area that looked like something out of a fairytale movie.

I was walking on an aisle of green, alpine grass and to my right was a slow-moving brook flowing south. It was like a Disneyland setting that was very magical. I continued on towards State Lakes. I took off my pack and rested. I thought about George and hoped that he got out ok with the firefighters. I decided to stay there overnight and leave back to Granite Lake the following day. I had a strange, daunting feeling about the place. It must have been because of that near-death experience that George and I went through, I thought. I tried to dismiss it by just going to sleep as fast as I could and not think about it.

STATE LAKES

I woke up seeing the raindrops dripping off the top of my tent. I unzipped the front opening and noticed that it was foggy, cold and the soil around me was wet. I hoped that the rain put out the forest fire. I looked up towards the sky and it was cloudy with a slight drizzle coming down. I felt lost, alone and cold but remembered that it was much worse on my first solo backpack trip when I walked down that water drainage, thinking it was a trail. I had to remind myself that it was part of the 'wilderness experience' and to just enjoy it as much as possible. I laid back on my sleeping bag and tried to sleep a bit more and wait for the sun. I dozed off and the sun woke me up as it hit my tent. I looked outside my tent and the sun burned off the fog. I got out and heated my water for coffee. I didn't see or hear anyone around. State Lakes in definitely not a popular spot for backpackers. I thought about the family group that gave George and me a big breakfast and that made me want to hurry up and see them again. I would tell them everything that happened and they would offer me another meal, I hoped. I pulled out a protein bar and that was my breakfast with my coffee. I packed up and started my way back towards Granite Pass.

GRANITE LAKE….again

After going over the Pass, I picked up my pace hoping to see the family group again. I could smell the bacon and eggs in my mind. When I got to the family group area…..they were gone. The horse packer, his mules, and horses came and must have picked them up. I was disappointed but not really surprised because of the forest fire that was nearby. I looked to the west and saw that the fire smoke was gone. I went to the same campsite on Granite Lake that George and I stayed at earlier and pitched my tent. I wanted to stay there one more night before heading back down and start hitchhiking back home. I sat on a grassy area and leaned back on a large boulder contemplating my situation. I had been on life-threatening situations before but the forest fire was the most frightful experience I've ever been in. I thought about my Mom and Dad, Pablo, Nick, and other close friends that I had in college. I realized that it is so easy to die up here in the wilderness if you aren't careful. I'll never take fire smoke for granted anymore when I am backpacking. I looked up to the sky and thanked God that he was with me and George. I asked Him to walk with me and choose my path wherever I roam. I prayed until I fell asleep.

The next morning, I woke up to the sound of water splashing and men laughing. I looked out and saw two men wading in the lake. When I got out of my tent, I saw six more men in that family group site camping there. They were all firefighters, resting, no doubt, from their hard work putting out that fire yesterday. I packed up my gear and, on the way out, asked them if they had any information on George, after I told them what happened.

"I'll check on that" one of the firefighters said.

He pulled out his radio and called in to headquarters to check.

"Yes, your friend is ok. He said he could drive and decided to go see his doctor, so he drove home." the firefighter said.

I thanked him and got back on the Copper Creek Trail for home.

It was a hard hike down the mountain to Road's End. I stopped a few times to take a break from the painful pounding on my knees from the weight of my body and pack. When I got down to the parking lot, I stopped and sat on a bench on a hill just above the lot. I saw a park ranger drive by slowly checking to see if everything was ok with all visitors. After a lunch of nuts, cranberries, and water, I stood by the edge of the road and started to motion my right thumb out in a hitchhiker's position every time I would see a car drive by. I continued to walk slowly down the road and waited for another car. There weren't too many cars going out. I kept walking and then saw that same park ranger driving up the road. He saw that I was dirty and tired and stopped.

"Hi, there. Are you ok, buddy?" he asked.

"Yes, sir…..just hoping to get a ride home after my partner left me stranded when he got sick with the forest fire smoke up at Granite Basin." I said.

"Oh, ok…..but hitchhiking is not allowed on Park Service land." he said.

"But that's the only way I can get home. He took the car." I said.

"Get in my car and I'll take you to where it's legal to hitchhike." he said.

I got into his car and he drove me to the borderline of the Park Service and the Forest Service. There was a nice campsite on Forest Service land and he stopped his car.

"You can hitchhike from here and it's legal." the park ranger said as he smiled.

"Do you have any food left or any money?" he said.

"I have one more day of food…..no money." I said.

 I got out of his car and grabbed my pack. When I sat on a log by the camp, he walked up to me and gave me a twenty-dollar bill.

"That's in case the driver that picks you up asks you for gas money." he said.

I couldn't believe it. What a great guy this man was. I noticed his name tag and I told him I will send him a check when I get home. I thanked him and he left.

After a few hours, a car stopped and I got a ride all the way home, since he lived in Three Rivers too. He never asked for gas money……just wanted friendly conversation. I thought that there are so many great people that come to visit in these beautiful mountains and park rangers too. I plan on seeing many more soon. I looked up to the sky and thanked the Lord for taking care of me. I was hoping to hear that raven fly above me but I guess the fire smoke chased him away.

Harrison Hawk

Sequoia Mountain Man

(a book of Adventures in the Wild – episode 10)

by

Connor Corkill

FRANKLIN SAWTOOTH LOOP

HITCHHIKING

I called Nick to see if he could give me a ride back up to Mineral King Valley to see Franklin Lakes but he told me that he was drafted into the army. They told him that he would leave to Viet Nam after he passes the physical. I told him that I was sorry to hear that, since he and I had joined in protest marches in the past.

At the junction of Hwy 198 and Mineral King Road, I stood by the road trying to get a ride up to Mineral King Valley by hitchhiking. There weren't too many people going up that road. Some drivers didn't have room for me, some weren't going that far, or some drivers were afraid to add a stranger into their vehicle. Nevertheless, I felt someone would pick me up. I stood there for six hours until an old Winnebago RV pulled over. It only had four small wheels on that big rusty RV. The side door opened and a heavy-set woman in her 70's smiled and asked me where I was going. I told her and she told me they were also going there. I entered her side door and she had a huge Great Dane staring at me. He didn't bark but he kept his eye on me. The lady's husband, or so I thought, was driving and told me to join him up front. He looked about the same age as the lady. I put my pack down and sat on the passenger seat. He was very nice and welcomed me aboard. What was strange was that he had a parrot, or cockatoo, not sure which, perched up on his steering wheel. I asked him if he had ever been on that road and he said "no". I told him that there were over 600 turns going up and that his parrot might fly off. He said that the parrot wouldn't mind the turns. We were on our way and every time the driver turned the steering wheel the parrot would adjust by moving his feet so that he was always on the top of the wheel. When the man would turn left, the parrot would move to the right and vice versa, always making sure he was upright. It was funny to see but a bit dangerous, since there were many areas where we could go over the cliff because the old RV would sway back and forth with every turn.

We made it all the way into the Mineral King Valley and I thanked them for the ride. I checked into a campsite at Cold Springs Campground and I should be acclimated by morning. I walked to the ranger station and got my 'permit' and planned to leave early morning, since it will be a long hike to Franklin Lakes.

FRANKLIN LAKES

I woke up at dawn and ate my last big meal for breakfast.....two hard-boiled eggs, a 4-ounce block of cheese, a thick slice of ham between two slices of bread with two cups of coffee. I was now ready to go to Franklin Lakes, over the Pass to Forester Lake, then to Soda Creek, and finish the loop coming back over Sawtooth Pass, which I had already seen on the Black Rock Pass Loop.

I walked alongside the East Fork of the Kaweah River and soon passed by the horse corral on my left. There were two unsaddled horses in the corral but no humans in sight. I continued on until I got to a stand of aspen trees. They were absolutely beautiful with their golden leaves shimmering in the wind. One side of the leaves were more golden than the other side and they seemed to glitter like ornaments on a Christmas tree when the wind blows. I sat among them for awhile then marched on. Right after crossing Franklin Creek, I started climbing about twenty switchbacks as I walked beside the deep Franklin Canyon. When I got to the Franklin Lakes and Farewell Gap junction, I was out of drinking water. I saw an area with a few ferns among the granite rock that was about 100 yards away and decided to check if there was water there. I took off my T-shirt, which was soaked with sweat and spread it out on a large boulder to dry while I went to filter water. When I got back, my T-shirt was torn to shreds. I realized that the marmots in the area smelled the salt of my sweat and started feasting on my shirt. I put it back in my pack and will use it as a rag. I put on a clean, dry T-shirt and walked east to Franklin Lakes. As I passed a rock slide area full of shattered granite, I saw something lying about fifty yards away. I looked through my monocular and saw that it was a carcass of a young buck. It had three-point antlers on each side and half of his body was missing. It looked like a bear caught up to him and ate part of his body. I continued on and saw a hole in the mountain big enough to walk in. It was the Lady Franklin Mine. It was mined for silver or some other metal ore many years ago. I didn't walk into it but went to the opening to see how deep it was. It wasn't very deep. From there I could see the Franklin Dam and a nice campground just below the lake. I hurried to get a campsite, since there was no one in sight. When I got there, I chose the only one that had a small tree for shade. I pitched my tent and rested for 30 minutes. The dam was holding all the water from the lower Franklin Lake. I walked to the creek that was created by an opening below the dam. The creek was a perfect place to filter water into my canteens and to rinse off my body. After getting cleaned up, I went back to my camp and saw a group of backpackers walking up to my area. I could see that the lead man was staring at me and seemed agitated about something. He walked up to me, huffing and puffing, and he seemed mad about something.

"I had this area reserved for my group" he said.

I looked at him and almost started to laugh.

"Sir, you can't reserve campsites in the wilderness." I corrected him.

"Yes, you can…….I have a group here and I want these campsites for us." he demanded.

"I will be happy to share this area with your group. There's enough room here for four or five more tents, but I'm not going to break down my camp and move away to another camp just because you want my campsite." I told him.

By that time, the other backpackers in his group gathered around. I explained to them that people can't make other campers move. It's 'first come, first served', I explained. Another man in the group pulled the angry man aside and talked to him. More members of the group joined in on the discussion. I just sat on a boulder by my tent and waited to see what they decided to do. The group didn't say another word and they all started to walk away to campsites above the dam.

The next day, on my way to the Pass, I looked down from the trail and saw the angry man laughing and joking to other members of the group. They were having breakfast and all seemed to be having a good time. The angry man looked up at me, smiled, and waved at me. I waved back and was glad everything turned out OK.

BEAR ATTACK

The trail up to Franklin Pass was excellent. It was very wide and not so steep because the switchbacks were constructed professionally. Halfway up the switchbacks, I looked back and saw the upper Franklin Lake, which was almost as big as the lower one. When I got up to the Pass, I was amazed at the view. I could see Florence Peak behind me, Forester Lake down below, and Rattlesnake Canyon and Shotgun Pass to my right. The trail switched to my left for about twenty yards and I started the descent at that point. The granite sand was hard and gradual on the way down. When I was halfway to Rattlesnake Canyon, I saw a beautiful lake off the cliff on my left but it didn't look like any camping spots were available there. I walked another thirty yards and looked over another cliff and there was a very flat and large plateau with brooks meandering through the middle of it. I got down to Rattlesnake Canyon and refilled my canteens at Rattlesnake Creek. It was only 2.2 miles from the Pass. I then walked down the canyon until I got to a junction with a sign that said 'Forester Lake' with an arrow pointing to the left. I hiked up and as I was halfway to the lake, I saw a bear cub climbing a tree about twenty yards away. I stopped and tried not to make a sound because I knew that mama bear was close by. But then I heard what I dreaded to hear......the cub cried out after seeing me. I turned around and saw mama bear charging towards me on my right side. My heart started pounding and I threw myself to the ground and covered the back of my head with my hands. I knew she was going to attack me. My face was in the ground and my backpack was the only thing protecting my torso. The bear growled as she slapped by backpack and kept her paw on it so I wouldn't get up. I froze and didn't make a sound hoping she wouldn't kill me. Mama bear held her paw on my backpack for a few minutes, which seemed like a few hours. She then let go. I heard branches shuffling and then silence. I didn't dare move for another five or ten minutes. I finally had the courage to peek out and noticed that she and her cub were gone. My heart was still racing. I waited for my heart rate to get back to normal. I slowly got up and looked all around before walking up the trail. I don't think my heart stopped beating fast enough until I got into camp at Forester Lake. I checked my backpack and noticed a tear of about four inches, compliments of mama bear. I was hoping one of her claws had fallen off so I could have it as a souvenir and then brag about it to Pablo and Nick, but no luck finding a claw around. All I had was the tear on my backpack to prove it.

FORESTER LAKE

Forester Lake was a beautiful lake. I chose to make a camp on the east side of the lake, which is usually the camp for horse riders. I could tell it was meant for them because of the hitching post near the camp. It had a small sandy beach and I could see trout swimming by the edge of the lake. The view I had from that point was 180 degrees of peaks, including Shotgun Pass, Franklin Pass, and other unnamed peaks to the west. About fifty yards to the north of my campsite, there was a dumping sewer hole with three walls of five-foot fencing for privacy. There was plenty of dry wood for making a fire, which I gathered and stacked near the fire pit. I now had enough for two nights. Since mama bear now knows that I'm near the area, she might visit me with hopes to get some of my food. I made sure that I would hang my food high and make it secure. I chose a branch about twenty feet high and not too strong because mother bears teach their cubs to climb the tree, walk along the branch and tear the rope with its tiny claws. I made sure that the branch would not be able to hold the weight of the cub.

That first night was cold with clear skies. The fire in the pit kept me warm and the stars were absolutely breathtaking. They seemed to glitter and twinkle as they would fade in and out with the breeze of the night. The crackling of the fire calmed my soul and eased my mind, helping me forget the danger that I felt earlier in the day.

The next morning, I woke up to a heavy fog floating over the lake. It was cloudy and the peaks were obscured by the low clouds. I restarted the fire and brought down my food from the tree branch. I heated water for my coffee and oatmeal and waited for the sun to shine through. I relaxed after eating my breakfast and the sun finally burned out the fog hovering over the lake. I put together a day pack of nuts and dried fruit and started my day hike to the beautiful plateau that I saw when I was hiking down from the Pass.

I climbed a hill on the north side of the lake and when I got to the top, I walked to the west. Even though there was no trail, I knew that the plateau was in that direction. It was a sprawling field of alpine grasses with brooks flowing with water. It was magical. I walked the perimeter of the plateau and on the far side there was a small tree. I sat on the grass and had my lunch. After an hour of meditation and relaxation, I finished the perimeter and walked back to my camp. When I got back there was a group of backpackers on the opposite side of my campsite. They saw me and waved. I waved back. Looking through my monocular, I saw two men and two women. I did not approach them and they kept to themselves. One of the men started casting his fishing line out on the lake. I was a bit tired from my day hike so I rested under the shade of some lodgepole trees and took a nap. I woke up an hour or two later and it was dusk. I looked across the lake and the group had a large fire going in their fire pit. I thought their fire was too big and it reminded me of my Granite Pass forest fire experience that I went through. It was still fresh in my mind.

SODA CREEK

The next morning, I packed up my bag and left early towards Soda Creek. The hiking group across the lake was still there with their two tents still in place. I walked over yesterdays hill, went over it and down to Little Claire Lake. It was another beautiful lake that was about as big as Forester Lake. Half of it was surrounded by granite and the other half had trees with campsites spread out on the east side. I walked to the north end and saw Soda Creek about 500 feet below from where I was standing on the cliff. I hiked down the many switchbacks and finally crossed the shallow creek. I continued to hike the long, straight and narrow trail. I didn't see any good campsites until about halfway to the Lost Canyon junction. I didn't want to camp there. I had just hiked about 5 miles. When I got to the junction of Lost Canyon, I stopped for a water break and then continued through Lost Canyon on my way out over Sawtooth Pass.

COLUMBINE LAKE

I started climbing the granite trail from the west end of Lost Canyon. When I got to Columbine Lake, I was exhausted. I had already hiked over 12 miles. I decided to stay overnight behind a large boulder to block the wind. I still had plenty of water in my canteens. After pitching my tent, the breeze started getting stronger. I had to put large rocks over my tent lines to hold the tent from blowing away in case the wind got stronger. The huge boulder where I pitched my tent was blocking the wind pretty good. The wind was getting colder and stronger so I got inside my tent and didn't come out. During the middle of the night, I felt the wind moving my tent and it got so strong that my rain fly came undone on one side of the tent. It was flapping back and forth, making an awful loud sound as it whipped on the fabric of the tent. I thought my tent might blow off the mountain but I remembered that I was surrounded by big boulders. I looked to the top of my tent and saw the rain fly blow away. Looking through the mesh of my tent ceiling, the cold wind was blowing through and it was relentless. I stayed in my sleeping bag and zipped it all the way to the top and just prayed. I couldn't sleep at all that night but for a couple of hours. The wind eventually subsided and dawn finally smiled on me.

I got out of my tent when the sun started to shine on me. It was still cold but the wind was gone. I looked for my rain fly but it was gone.....probably blew off the mountain but I was safe. I didn't even bother to have coffee or breakfast. I packed my bag and I was only twenty yards away from the Pass. I went over it and went down to Monarch Lake.

MONARCH LAKE

Monarch Lake was a large, flat area surrounded by medium-sized boulders that were scattered with about twenty-five yard spacing. It had many campsites and there were about seven or eight tents that were pitched. I saw four or five backpackers standing outside of their tents sipping on coffee or whatever they were drinking as I walked in from Sawtooth Pass. They waved at me and I waved back. I didn't want to head on down to the Valley right away. I put my backpack down on one of the empty campsites and rested for awhile. I pulled out my stove and heated some water for my first cup of coffee that morning. I took out an oatmeal cookie from my duffle bag and placed it on a ledge of the boulder that I was leaning against. I started heating my water and turned to retrieve my cookie and it was gone. I forgot to realize that Pikas, little mice-like rodents, are very sneaky and fast. I'll never see that cookie again so I'll just eat my granola with my coffee. After having two cups of coffee, I put things away, grabbed my backpack and went down to Mineral King Valley.

I thought about the very interesting things that happened to me on this trip and couldn't wait to tell my brother and my friend, Nick about them. As soon as I got down to the parking lot, I saw a guy that came down the mountain and was ready to drive down the winding road. I asked him for a ride and he said he would take me down. I was very lucky that I didn't have to stick out my thumb and hope for a ride. We had a nice conversation all the way down. I told him about the parrot on the steering wheel and we both laughed. I can't wait for more adventures in the Sierra Nevada Mountains.

HARRISON HAWK

Sequoia Mountain Man

(a book of short stories – episode 11)

by

Connor Corkill

SURVIVAL MODE

VERMILLION RESORT

My brother, Pablo, called me and told me about this place in the Kaiser Wilderness. He had a friend that worked at Vermillion Resort and he invited Pablo and me to visit so we could backpack the area, if we wanted to. His name was Jimmy and he said he would drive us there when he is supposed to start work there. Pablo and I agreed so I am starting my first backpack trip of the year in late July. We realized that it will be colder and we will see some snow in the higher peaks. Pablo and I planned on hiking the northern half of the John Muir Trail all the way to Yosemite.

We started our car trip from Fresno and drove past Huntington Lake and eventually to the one-lane road to the resort. Jimmy told us that Edison Lake was very popular with fishermen and that it was also a stopover for John Muir Trail backpackers. They can mail their food and supplies to the resort because it was close to the middle of the 211-mile JMT. He said that the resort has a good restaurant that served large portions of food. Another reason that backpackers loved it there was because they would get a free overnight stay in a large tent reserved for them. Jimmy said that he would arrange for Pablo and me to stay in that large canvas tent when we get there and we won't have to pitch our tents anywhere.

We arrived in the late afternoon and Jimmy told us to choose which cots we wanted and to lay our backpacks on them, that way we will claim those cots for the night. We walked to the restaurant with Jimmy. He told us he was one of the cooks in the kitchen. Pablo ordered a dinner plate and I ordered a cheeseburger with fries. Both meals were very good, mainly because of the quantity of food. After eating, we went back to our tent and went to sleep early.

THE FERRY

In the middle of the night, we heard someone making noise outside our tent. I looked out and saw a backpacker breathing hard and pulling out his stove to heat some water. He must have hiked during the night and had just come in. I went back to sleep and let him enjoy his meal or coffee.

We woke up just before dawn, repacked our gear and went to the restaurant for some coffee and breakfast. The restaurant was just opening up and Pablo and I were the first ones there. We ordered coffee and pancakes. Jimmy was working the morning shift so he gave us a big plate with three huge pancakes for each. When we were through eating, we went to the main store to buy our passes for the ferry. The ferry would save us a long hike of 7 miles to get to the opposite side of the lake. Our backpacks weighted about 50 lbs. each, including food.

We boarded the ferry along with four other backpackers. They said they were hiking south along the John Muir Trail to Mt. Whitney. It was cold and the moon was still shining bright on that clear, crisp morning. The old man that was in charge of the ferry was very friendly and told us a few stories about the experiences that other backpackers have had. By the time we got to the end of the lake, the sun was peeking out over the pine trees on the east side. As we unloaded our packs from the ferry, there were three other backpackers that had been waiting for the ferry to take them to the resort.

We started our hike about two miles from Quail meadows. We now know why they called it Quail Meadows after seeing a mother quail leading her ten little chicks across the trail. We passed the junction that would take us east alongside Mono Creek. We went north towards Pocket Meadow. When we came to a junction that divides the JMT with the trail to Mott Lake, we followed the JMT on our way to Silver Pass Lake.

CLIFF MEADOW

After passing Pocket Meadow, we saw that our trail was leading us to a high 200-foot cliff. We hiked up that cliff to a meadow. There was no name for that meadow on our map so Pablo and I called it Cliff Meadow. It was a beautiful meadow and on the northeast side was a long, smooth slab of granite next to a shady campsite. We decided to stay there, since it had a firepit and plenty of dry wood for making a fire. We made ourselves comfortable and we were delighted to have such a great campsite.

"Our next camp will be Silver Pass Lake and I hope it's as nice as this." I said.

"No, because we won't be able to make a fire up there since it's over 10,000 feet and I like a warm fire in our campsite." Pablo said.

After relaxing for about two hours, we noticed four horse riders that came up the cliff to the meadow. I looked through my monocular and saw that one of them was a woman. They noticed us and came to say hello. They were friendly and said they were going over the Pass to Helen Lake to do some fishing and will be going back to Edison Lake in a few days. They left after a brief conversation with us. I'm glad we made some friends. We can help each other sometimes if we need to.

We had enough food for about nine more days and we thought that would be plenty until we reach Yosemite. We decided to stay an extra night, since it was such a great campsite. We gathered wood for the fire and it was good weather. We walked the perimeter of the meadow and we thoroughly enjoyed our stay there.

The next morning, we looked out of our tents and noticed a fog hovering over the meadow. It was cold so Pablo started the fire again to keep us warm while we had our usual coffee and oatmeal for breakfast.

"I kind of hate to leave this great campsite, bro." Pablo said.

"Yes, it's been a great camp but we can't stay another night." I said.

THE RAVEN

As we were breaking camp, a raven flew from over the meadow and perched itself on a red fir branch by our campsite.

"What's a raven doing here at over 9,000 feet elevation?" I asked.

Pablo just stared at it and didn't say a word. He stood up and walked towards the back bird. He started mumbling some prayers that I couldn't understand. The raven kept staring t him then flew away. It was eerie as the mysterious bird started cawing as he flew away.

"What was that all about?" I asked.

"Sometimes the raven knows things that will happen and warns us." Pablo said.

"I'm not superstitious, Pablo" I said.

Pablo looked at me and didn't say a word.
We packed our gear and started hiking up the mountain.

Silver Pass Lake

When we got to the lake, we found a rectangular granite slab that was about two feet high and perfect to sit on. Our two tents fir perfectly beside it. The only problem was that there was no shade at all, so we were exposed to the elements. There were patches of snow all around us, which made it colder when the breeze blew towards us. There were a few bristlecone pines around but were very small and they couldn't supply any shade. Everything looked OK except for not having any shade or having a fire to keep us warm.

"That's OK...we're leaving in the morning anyway, so one night won't hurt." I said.

Pablo looked at me and slowly nodded his head.

That afternoon, I started getting the stove and fuel ready to start dinner. Pablo went for a walk to see the area. I was hoping we wouldn't get a visit from a bear because there was no place to hang our food on a tree branch. We will have to keep it inside our tents during the night. It would be unlikely to see a bear this high in elevation since there are no berries or anything else for him to eat. The only way we would see one is if he was crossing over from one side of the mountain to another.

While I started to heat the water in my stove, I saw Pablo limping back to camp. He couldn't put any weight on his right leg and was dragging it. I put the food away and went to help him back to camp.

"What happened, bro?" I asked.

"I slipped walking on a boulder and smashed my right knee. It might be my knee cap but I'm not sure." he said.

I noticed there was also a tear on his pants and blood was soaking through. I helped him to sit on the boulder by our tents and pulled out my first aid kit. I rolled up his pant leg to see the damage. There was a gash and blood oozing out. I pressed on his knee to stop the bleeding while he took a roll of gauze out of the first aid kit. I firmly kept my hand on his knee until the bleeding finally stopped. I could tell he was in pain so I gave him a pain pill from the kit. We wrapped the knee with gauze and hoped that there would be no swelling. I walked to a patch of snow and filled our food pan with it. I put the snow in my bandana, wrapped it tight and pressed it on the wound, hoping that would lessen the swelling. Pablo took over by pressing the snow-filled bandana on the wound. There was nothing else we could do except hope for the best.

I made pasta on my stove for both of us that evening. We ate and then the wind started picking up so we got inside our tents and didn't come out for the rest of the night. It was a clear night and the stars above us were so bright that I could see the Milky Way in all its glory. The wind was blowing on our tents but not hard enough to blow them away. I prayed that night that everything would be all right in the morning and then I fell asleep.

The next morning, I could hear Pablo moaning in his sleep.
I got up and asked him if he was awake. He didn't answer so I
figured he was still asleep but in pain. I noticed that the cloudy
skies were now turning darker and I thought we might start
having some rain soon. I hurried to finish making breakfast
before it would start pouring. Pablo woke up to the smell of
coffee.

"How do you feel, bro?" I asked.

"About the same.....I think it's either a knee cap or I pulled a
tendon but not sure." he answered.

I gave him a cup of coffee and he stayed inside his tent.

"I'm making breakfast. Stay inside because it might start raining
soon. Some rain clouds are forming and moving in." I said.

I thought that if he broke his knee cap, then our trip is over.
We'll be lucky to get out by the way we came in. I handed him
his oatmeal and protein bar. I started heating my water for my
coffee and oatmeal when it started sprinkling. The water was
only lukewarm when it started raining, so I put things away and
went in my tent. My lukewarm coffee and protein bar were my
breakfast. All of a sudden, we started hearing rolling thunder.
The rain started pouring harder and harder. We were dry inside
our tents. All of a sudden, we heard an extremely loud thunder
clap. It was so deafening that it hurt my ears. It felt like lightning
struck right by us. I looked out my tent and saw lightning
flashing in the sky. I yelled out to Pablo asking if he was OK. He
didn't answer. The thunder got louder....another lightning strike
hit a boulder on one of the peaks and I saw smoke rising from
that boulder. I quickly zipped up my tent and started praying. It

was so scary. We stayed inside our tents for the rest of the day and night.

The next morning, I woke up and felt water under the floor of my tent. I was so glad that my North Face tent didn't let any water inside. I looked outside and it was partly cloudy and there were water puddles all around us. I took out my stove and fuel and started heating water for coffee and breakfast. I called out to Pablo.

"Pablo, are you OK?" I asked.

"Yes, I'm fine but my knee is very stiff. I can't bend it." he answered.

"Is it still swollen?" I asked again.

"Yes, it's still swollen and I'm seeing bruising too." he said.

That was not good news. I knew that we had to go back to Edison Lake soon.....but how and when, I thought. I counted our food and we only had enough for 6 days left, including today. I helped Pablo get out of his tent and he sat on that flat boulder for the rest of the morning. I found a 'wrap' and gently started wrapping his knee but it was too painful so I stopped. Pablo said that it would be better to wrap it after the swelling goes down.....but when would that be.

In the afternoon, we saw that horse group of four coming over the Pass. I was overjoyed that they might help us. I waved them in and I told them what happened to Pablo and that we needed help.

"I can take him on my horse down to the ferry." the woman said.

I looked at Pablo, smiled and nodded because we were getting help now.

"What about my backpack?" Pablo said.

"You'll have to leave it here and pick it up later. We have no way of tying it on our riding horses." one of the men said.

Pablo shook his head and said he won't leave his pack here unattended for days. He thanked them for offering help but said he'll just wait till the swelling goes down and walk back to the ferry. They understood and left.

"Bro, that might have been the only way for you to get down." I said.

"You can't carry both backpacks so you'd have to leave mine up here for days. Bears would come, tear it apart, eat the food and destroy the rest of it." he said.

We stayed pretty quiet for the rest of the day. I took a walk around the alpine grasses with medium-sized boulders protruding out from the meadow. I stayed within eye distance of Pablo in case he needed help. When I got back to camp, I heated water and added freeze-dried beans for our dinner. I was glad that it didn't rain that day. We went to bed early and hoped that the swelling would go down by tomorrow.

THE MOUNTAIN LION

The next morning, I laid out some wet clothes over the small trees nearby so they could dry out with the sun starting to shine on us. It soon started getting too hot by the middle of the day and there was no shade on our camp. I looked out to the grassy meadow and saw a mountain lion. I immediately stood up and alerted Pablo, who was sitting on the camp boulder. I yelled out and waved my hands to shoo him away. The lion looked at me and walked away slowly…..very slowly.

"Maybe he smells your blood that might still be on that boulder, bro." I said.

"It should be all gone by now after that rain we had 2 days ago." Pablo said

"Yeah…..maybe." I said.

I continued on with my daily chores of cooking food and trying make things easier for Pablo while still keeping an eye out for the lion. The sun was getting hotter and hotter. It started burning our skin so we had to wear long-sleeved shirts and long pants even though it was too hot for them to wear. Now we were hoping for clouds to move in and cool us down but there wasn't a cloud in sight. I made a mistake by heating ramen noodles for dinner and knew that the lion could smell it and return. I apologized to Pablo about that but he waved it off. I rinsed the pot really well in the lake and hoped the lion wouldn't come during the night. We retired at dusk and hoped the knee would get better.

We woke up to another clear and sunny day. The day was going to be just like the last day….with the scorching sun and here we are without shade all day long. After making breakfast, I looked up and saw the lion watching us.

"That lion is stalking us, bro." I said.

"He knows we have food and is not going away." I continued.

"There is only one thing we can do, my brother." Pablo said.

"We are fighting the hot sun and now the lion who won't go away so we have to go back down to Cliff Meadow." Pablo continued.

We decided that I would pack my tent and gear in the morning and leave down to Cliff meadow, set up camp there and on the following morning, I would walk back up to Silver Pass Lake camp, put Pablo's backpack on my back and take it to Cliff Meadow, pitch Pablo's tent, then walk up again on the same day and help Pablo walk slowly down the mountain to Cliff Meadow where there is shade and no lion. That was the plan.

"Yes, we have to do it. Not only because of the sun and lion but we are running out of food." I said.

The next morning, I heated water and made breakfast for both of us. I also gave Pablo dry jerky and nuts for his dinner that afternoon. I refilled our canteens and I started hiking down the mountain to Cliff Meadow. When I got there, I was glad to see that the campsite that we had before was vacant. I quickly pitched my tent, hung my food on a tree branch, gathered wood for a fire and have it all set up for us. I didn't go back to see Pablo that day because I would have to walk up again, bring his backpack down, pitch his tent, then go back up again and help him walk down. It would be too much for me to handle. Pablo knew this. He knew he would be alone that night.....with the lion.

I woke up before dawn, had coffee and a protein bar and walked up the mountain with only my canteen of water. On the way up, I found a dry, three-inch wide x 5-foot tree branch that was straight and would make a good crutch for Pablo when he would come down the mountain. I got to Silver Pass Lake around mid-morning and helped Pablo sit on the camp boulder. I packed up all his gear into his backpack, put it on my back and started down the mountain again. He would have to stay sitting on that boulder alone with just his canteen of water until I came back to help him down. When I got to Cliff Meadow, I pitched his tent, put his supplies inside his tent, consolidated our food and hung the bag on a tree branch. I then started walking up the mountain again. When I got there, he was still sitting on the boulder.

"Did the lion come back?" I asked.

"Yes, he's still around but it's getting really hot again." he said.

Before we started the walk down the mountain, I wrapped his knee with the first aid 'wrap'. He trimmed down the log crutch that he'll use and cushioned it with a sweat shirt to fit under his armpit. I put his left arm around my shoulder and we started down the mountain one hop after another.

It took us all day to get down the mountain. When we got there, I helped him to sit on a log where he was now in the shade and then I collapsed from exhaustion. I never felt so tired in my life. I fell asleep and didn't wake up until the next morning.

When we woke up, we just relaxed for most of the morning. Pablo noticed that the swelling was going down a bit but still had a lot of pain. He took a pain pill but saved the last two pills for the way down to the ferry. It would be a much longer walk. I noticed we only had two days of food left so we decided to rest one more day and then start hiking down to the ferry. That means that we would be out of food on the hike down. I looked in the first aid kit for anything that would help his knee. At the bottom of the kit, I found a small bottle of Tea Tree Oil. I was half empty but I was hoping it might help him. "Do you think this might help if you rub it inf?" I asked. "Maybe,,,,,,I'll try it." Pablo said

I handed him the bottle and he started rubbing it on his knee. We were so glad to get away from the hot sun, lion, thunderstorms, lightning, and rain at Silver Pass Lake, although it was very beautiful there. Resting for another day might help the swelling go down completely, we hoped. I kept looking around to see if that lion followed us to Cliff Meadow but I never saw him again. Later that day, we saw a herd of deer grazing in the grass of the meadow. If the deer, who have excellent hearing, were comfortable in the meadow, then maybe there was no danger of a lion or bear in the vicinity.

The next day was our last day at camp. We knew that we had no food left. No protein bars, oatmeal, pasta, nor freeze-dried fruit. We only had enough coffee for tomorrow morning, our day of departure. I saved a handful of nuts for us to have with our coffee tomorrow and we'll have to hope for the best because Pablo will have to hike down the mountain with his backpack on his back. Resting all day is the only thing we will do until tomorrow.

THE LONG WAY HOME

We woke up before sunrise. I spread out all our gear on my ground tarp and put all our supplies on it. I knew that I had to take all the heaviest gear on my backpack and make Pablo's backpack the lightest as possible, since he had to carry his own. I loaded all the cookware, tents, sleeping bags, and clothes inside and outside my pack. My backpack was now weighing about 70 pounds and Pablo's was about 25 pounds. Pablo only had two canteens of water, first-aid kit, and some nuts in his pack. Pablo took a sweatshirt and cushioned his crutch where it makes contact with his armpit. I wrapped his knee and we started our descent slowly into the cold, dark morning. When we got to the edge of the cliff, Pablo had a hard time hiking down. It took us three hours to get to the bottom. We still had a long way to go. Pablo was wincing in pain every few steps. He told me he had already taken the last of the pain pills but they weren't helping that much.

When we finally got to Quail Meadows, I noticed that it was already 4 o'clock and the ferry gets to the dock at 5 or 5:30 and leaves immediately after that. I had been walking slowly with Pablo all day long.

"Pablo, I think I should hurry to the dock so I can hold up the ferry because I don't think we'll get there in time at the pace we're going." I said.

"Yes, go on. I'll be OK." Pablo said.

I started to quicken my pace and left him at Quail Meadow. He could only take one step at a time and, even though I had 70 pounds on my back, I could walk a little faster.

It was 4:30 and I still had mile to go to the loading dock. I tried to go faster but the weight was really affecting my stamina. I had to stop from time to time to catch my breath and take the pain in my back. I tried to go faster but the tents on top of my pack were slipping off so I had to take off my pack and readjust the tents. I looked at my watch and it was fifteen minutes until 5 o'clock. I started yelling as I walked hoping the driver or another backpacker would hear me and hold up the ferry. I yelled "STOP, STOP" over and over again. When I could see the dock, I hurried faster and yelled again but then….I saw the ferry leaving. It was about fifty yards away on the lake and they couldn't hear my screaming because of the engine sounds, I thought. It was disheartening. I failed. I dropped my backpack on the ground and fell to my knees.

After a few minutes of rest to catch my breath, I knew I couldn't lament on my misfortune. I had to go help Pablo to get to the dock and wait for the ferry tomorrow morning. I took one of my tarps and laid it out on the shady grass by some small trees. I put my heavy backpack on it and covered it with Pablo's tarp. I then started to hike back to meet Pablo and help him. When I got to where Pablo was, he was in extreme pain. I took his backpack and put it on my back. I put his left arm around my shoulder, as I did when we were coming down Silver Pass Lake. We slowly but surely made it to the dock right around dusk. He already knew what happened. I didn't have to tell him.
"We'll have to sleep here overnight and get the ferry when it comes at 7:30 in the morning." I said.
"At least we got here, bro…..thanks to you." Pablo said in obvious pain.
I didn't pitch our tents, since there was no place to do it. I took out our two sleeping bags and laid them out. We will sleep under the stars for the last time on this trip.

In the morning, we waited anxiously for the ferry to pick us up. It was 7:30 and the ferry was still out of sight.

"What else can go wrong on this trip, bro" I said.

I reminded him about the raven that we saw at Cliff Meadow

"Yes, sometimes a raven can warn us of a coming disaster but they can also protect us from those disasters.....and I think that's what that raven did as I prayed while he was perched on that branch." Pablo said.

Just as he finished saying that, we could see the ferry coming toward us. We smiled and thanked God that everything will be OK now.

"Are you ready for some pancakes and hot coffee, bro?" I yelled out

This trip showed me that no matter what the negative circumstances are, we can overcome them if we put our minds into a 'survival mode'. Pablo and I found a ride back to Fresno, where we got on a Greyhound and finally completed the long way home.

Harrison Hawk

Sequoia Mountain Man

(a book of Adventures in the Wild - episode 12)

by

Connor Corkill

The Volcano

FAREWELL GAP TRAIL

There was a place off of Kern River that not too many people knew about. It was a place where a volcano erupted thousands of years ago and I wanted to see it, since it was now dormant. Pablo wanted to go with me, now that he has recovered from his knee problem that turned out to be nothing but a bruised bone and a sprained tendon. It was now September so he had almost two months to recover from that unfortunate accident.

We got a ride from Nick to Mineral King. Nick was lucky that he didn't have to go into the army because he was married and had a son so he was exempt from the draft. We drove to Cold Springs Campground and chose a nice campsite that was

secluded and surrounded by brush with a cliff behind us. Nick told us that he could only stay for two nights because he had to return to work. Pablo and I decided to stay at camp for those two nights with Nick, mainly because he was such a great cook and always brings good food. We enjoyed camping together and Pablo and I could acclimate fully before we start our climb.
"Make sure you take pictures of the volcano……I want to see it." Nick said.
"We will, Nick, and thank you so much for the ride." I said.
"If you can't get a ride back home, call me but make sure that it's a weekend because that's when I'm off work." Nick said.
"OK, buddy, take care." Pablo said and we started our hike.

    We picked up our hiking 'permit' at the ranger station and started our climb on Farewell Gap Trail. I was familiar with it, after my hike to Franklin Lakes last year. We passed the horse stables and stopped at Aspen Flats for awhile to enjoy the beauty of those shimmering golden leaves. After climbing the short switchbacks, we took a water break and rested for fifteen minutes and then continued on up. When we finally got to the lower Franklin Lake, we were lucky that there was no one at the same campsite that I had last year below the dam. We pitched our tents, rinsed our bodies and got comfortable. Pablo said he missed having a fire but they were not allowed here above 10,000 feet.
I told Pablo about the angry man that wanted to kick me out of my camp last year and he laughed.
"He might have been a 'flatlander'. Some of them don't know the rules or they think that they can break them to their advantage." Pablo said.

FRANKLIIN PASS

The next morning, we climbed past the two Franklin Lakes and when we stopped at the Pass, we saw an old man that looked like Santa Claus sitting on a boulder enjoying the view. He was a friendly old chap and he told us some stories of some places he had hiked in his lifetime. We enjoyed hearing his tales of adventures in the Sierra Nevada Mountains. He even chuckled like a Santa Claus in a city mall. After trading stories for 30 minutes, we headed on down to Rattlesnake Canyon, where we made a camp by Rattlesnake Creek. I told Pablo about 'mama bear' that attacked me the previous year not too far from where we were.

"Yes, that's when we should be afraid of a bear attack……when there is a cub around or when you surprise any bear, corner him and he feels trapped." Pablo said.

We started to make dinner when a rainfall surprised us. We both took our stoves inside our tents and we were careful heating up our water and cooking our ramen noodles. The rain was over in less than an hour and we had sunshine for the rest of the day. We knew we had a long hike tomorrow on Rattlesnake Canyon Trail until we would get to Kern River so we went to bed at dusk.

From here on out, everything would be new to me and to Pablo, so we kept our senses high on alert, especially me because of that mama bear that I kept thinking about. The trail was going downslope and it was pretty visible all the way. When we finally got down to Kern River, we were tired but lucky to see a very flat area right next to the river so we made camp there. There was a tall sycamore tree twenty yards away from our camp which had a high branch to hang our food. It was perfect. We saw a few backpackers go by, since we were camped between the river and the trail. Pablo gathered some dry wood and we had a nice fire that evening. We were at 6,585 feet in elevation, according to our map. The Kern River was moving pretty fast and it was still high, even though we were in September. There was a row of Sycamore trees across the river that lined up as if they were planted by man. We saw a red-tailed hawk perched high on one of the trees waiting to see if he could find a squirrel or other small mammal to scoop up.

The next morning, we had a very pleasant cup of coffee and a good breakfast of scrambled eggs and bacon from the Mountain House brand. After eating our food, we packed up and started our hike down the Kern River trail towards the National Park Service ranger station. As we passed Funston Meadow, we looked to our left and saw two men chopping some wood with an axe but they had uniforms on. They looked like they were part of a trail maintenance crew and were probably camped somewhere nearby. We didn't stop to talk so we just kept going south.

KERN RIVER RANGER STATION

When we got to the ranger station, we saw a man on the roof hammering some nails on the shingles. He saw us and came down to welcome us. His name was Darwin and said that his wife, Cindy, was the ranger. She was in the station feeding their baby. He invited us into the station and we chatted for a few minutes.

"We came this way because we are hoping to see the volcano in the Golden Trout Wilderness." I said.

"Yes, well, when you cross the bridge over the Kern, you'll be out of the National Park and into the GTW." Cindy said.

"There is a nice campsite by the river that is just beyond our jurisdiction that you would really like." Darwin said.

"Great!.....can we make a fire there?" Pablo asked.

"Absolutely" Darwin answered.

We left the station and walked to the campsite that Darwin suggested. It was very flat, had a tree for shade, and it was right next to the river just beyond the Park Service boundary. The magnificent Tower Rock was across the river in front of us. We pitched our tents and picked up some dry wood for the firepit. I walked to the edge of the river and saw a small eddy of about 24 inches wide with a big trout in it. The rainbow trout was about 14 or 15 inches long. I told Pablo to come and see it. His eyes opened wide. He squatted down low, put his hand under the fish and scooped him up, throwing him into the ground of our camp.

"We've got a fish dinner tonight, bro." he said

Pablo cut and cleaned the fish and sliced out two large fillets, one for each of us. That fish was the freshest and tastiest trout that I've ever had, and Pablo didn't even need bait on a hook or a rod and reel. He is a true outdoorsman and survivalist. I heated some freeze-dried beans to accompany the fish and it was a perfect combination.

The next morning, after finishing our breakfast, we broke camp and headed for the bridge. It was a well-made and sturdy bridge that will take us over the Kern River and to the GTW. We climbed the steep trail and soon got to Volcano Falls, a waterfall of about twelve feet high. We kept climbing and got to Natural Bridge. We filled our canteens there from a spring where water was coming out of the volcanic rocks. That water was the coldest water that I have ever felt. It was so cold that my hands were hurting from it. I wondered why it wasn't frozen. I guess it's one of those nature mysteries that are hard to explain.

THE VOLCANO

Just beyond passing the Natural Bridge, we started seeing a field of volcanic rock spread out over a large area. It was of a rustic red color and the sizes were from small rocks the size of potatoes to large rocks of about 18 inches wide. I picked one up and it was very light. There are different types of volcanic rock and I think this type was Pumice, because of the density. It was so light in weight that I could hold a large one with my hand and hold it with my arm extended outward. I was glad that the volcanic rocks were removed from the trail so we wouldn't have to walk over them. With pine trees all around us, we came to a fork on the trail where we hike to the volcano. We soon came to a large, beautiful green meadow at the base of the volcano. We started looking for a campsite, so we walked the perimeter of the meadow starting counterclockwise. We circled the meadow and couldn't find an adequate campsite. Just as we were completing our 360 degrees of the meadow, we saw a large one that was huge. It was obvious that it was used by horsemen, after seeing horseshoe prints all around. There was also a very high branch where we could hang our food nearby. We pitched our tents and made ourselves at home.

The next morning, we woke up to a partly cloudy day with a cold wind blowing over the meadow. After drinking two cups of coffee and a hearty breakfast, we closed our tents and started our climb to the top of the volcano. There was a trail that circled around to the east side of the volcano and we started climbing that steep trail. The volcanic rocks on the trail were much smaller in diameter than the ones we saw earlier coming up.

When we got to the orifice of the volcano, we looked down into the crater and saw two or three pine trees growing at the very bottom of the crater. It was strange to see that but the volcano was real. It was a small volcano but very real. Pablo and I congratulated each other and we took pictures for Nick to see when we'll get back home. We did not intend to go down into the crater. We couldn't tell how solid the volcanic rock was beyond the orifice and it might sink us into the deep or sink our boots to the point of not being able to climb out of it . After taking pictures, we descended the prehistoric tinderbox back to our camp.

"We met our goal, brother, now we can take our time going back home." I said.

"Harry, I can't wait to see Coyote Pass. I heard that it looks like those rocks that stand on each other like at Arches National Park in Utah." Pablo said.

"We can hike down to the ranger station tomorrow. It's all downhill." I reminded him.

"Yes, and maybe we'll be lucky to see another trout trapped in that eddy." Pablo said.

We left early the next morning on the way down, we each took a small volcanic rock to show Nick how light they were. I took one that was as big as a medium-sized potato and Pablo took a much bigger one.

"One thing for sure is we can't use them as 'paperweights'" I said.

We got down to the bridge around mid-afternoon and claimed our favorite campsite. There was no trout in the eddy so we just cooked our freeze-dried pasta and peas. After dinner, we went to say goodbye to Cindy and Darwin. Darwin was taking care of the baby while Cindy went on patrol on her horse. We said our goodbyes and started the climb up the trail by Coyote Creek.

COYOTE PASS

The Coyote Pass Trail was steep and long. It was semi-shady all the way up the trail. When we got to the fork where a trail could lead us to Coyote Lakes, Pablo wanted to see them but it would be a 12-mile round trip hike from where we were. We decided to forego that idea and continue on to the Pass.

When we got to the Pass, I realized what Pablo said was right on. There were huge rocks balancing on small rocks just like they do in Utah and Arizona. They were of a reddish-golden color, mainly because the sunset rays were shining right on them when we got there. Since the elevation was at 10,455, fires were not allowed on any campsite so Pablo wanted to go down where we can have a fire in our camp. Even though we were very tired, I agreed to it and we went down until we saw Rifle Creek. We looked for a campsite and the only one we found was hidden between some manzanita plants. It wasn't even a campsite but we squeezed in anyway because we were extremely exhausted since hiking nonstop from Kern River Ranger Station.

After eating 'dry' with 'turkey jerky' and nuts, dark clouds were forming above us and it started sprinkling quickly. We rushed into our tents. Pablo left his saucepan out in the open and upside down. Within a few seconds, it started hailing hard. I looked up to the roof of my tent and could see the indentations that the hail was making on it. I was expecting the hail to go right through my tent roof and start bombarding me with those golf-ball-sized hail on my body. As quickly as the torrent attacked us, it passed away just as fast. Pablo and I peeked out of our tents and Pablo saw his saucepan with dents on the bottom of it.

"That was some heavy hail that greeted us, bro." Pablo said.

"Yes, I'm glad it didn't last long." I said.

The next day, we hiked past Pistol Creek without even stopping for a break. We got to the junction to Silver Lake and continued on to our last camp of the trip, Bullion Flats.

BUILLION FLATS

When we were getting close to Bullion Flats, we noticed something hanging from a tree right over one of the campsites. I looked into my monocular but still couldn't figure out what it was. As we got closer, we noticed it was a large meshed net made of nylon. In it was about 100 empty cans of dog food. We couldn't realize why someone was hanging it about fifteen feet above the campsite. Looking around, we didn't see any other campers until Pablo pointed towards Farewell Gap.
"Up there.....I see some guys camping on a flat near the Gap." Pablo said.
I looked through my monocular and saw three men with bows and arrows.
"Oh, my God, there are three bow hunters up there." I said.
"Yes, I had forgotten that we're at the end of September and it's bow hunting season in the Golden Trout Wilderness." Pablo said.
"So THEY were the ones that put up this net....using it as bait?" I asked.
"Yes, bro, and we're camping right next to it." Pablo answered.
We chose a campsite that was the farthest one from the net. I looked up at the hunters and saw two of them looking at us with their binoculars.

"They probably know a bear or any other animal won't come to our camp while we're here so I'm pretty sure they don't like us being here." Pablo said.

We noticed a large family of marmots had a den just above our campsite. They seemed to be unafraid of people because they kept coming toward us, hoping we would give them something to eat. The rodents were persistent but kept their distance. On Park Service land, it is against the rules to give human food to animals and that includes marmots but we are in Forest Service land so anything goes, including bow hunting. Of course, we weren't giving those large squirrels the last of our food so we just ignored them.

We gathered some dry wood and made a fire that evening and hoped that a bear would not smell the dog food cans and surprise us in the middle of the night.

BIG BLACKIE

In the morning, we made our usual coffee and oatmeal and, since we still had two days of food left, we discussed if we should stay another night or not because Pablo wanted to go see Bullfrog Lake, which was just across the creek. We decided to stay one more night, so we re-hung our food on a tree, put all our belongings inside our tents and hiked to Bullfrog Lake. When we got there, Pablo was turning over rocks by the creek looking for souvenirs of silver nuggets or trinkets left by miners of the past century. I was looking at the bow hunters because we had a clear view of seeing their campsite from the Lake. They kept looking up at us too. After an hour or two, we went back to camp. Pablo didn't have any success of finding anything but we enjoyed the hike.

When we got back to our camp, we were gathering some more wood for our last campfire of the trip when suddenly we saw a huge black bear running towards us from over Vandever Mountain, which is adjacent to Farewell Gap on the west side. We were shaking in our pants because he was running hard. "He hasn't seen us yet." Pablo said.
"He must smell the dog food cans or smelled our food." I said. We stood up and waved our arms when he was about fifty yards away. He finally saw us and stopped on his tracks. He was surprised to see us and started walking to his left, keeping his eye on us. He crossed the creek and went up the slope and into the woods. I looked at the bow hunters and all three of them had their bows on the ready with metal-pointed arrows in position. My heart stopped beating fast after a half-hour or so. We kept looking up to where the bear, who we called 'Big Blackie', disappeared to, in case he decided to continue his assault on our camp.

We decided to eat 'dry' again, being that Big Blackie might smell our cooking and appear again. We both made a large fire and kept it going all night long, since there was no wind and it might keep the big guy away. We both had a restless and uncomfortable sleep that night and couldn't wait for the sun to come up. At the break of dawn, we put out the fire, ate our breakfast as fast as possible and packed up and hiked towards Farewell Gap.

We never saw Big Blackie again and as we passed the bow hunters camp, we noticed that only one was keeping watch while the rest of the hunters were still asleep in their tents. We hiked over Farewell Gap and down to Mineral King Valley.

We had another adventurous backpack trip that started in Sequoia National Park, moved to The Golden Trout Wilderness, back to the Park, then again to the GTW, and finally back to the National Park. We will call Nick to pick us up tomorrow, since it will be Saturday. Pablo and I have had some momentous times in the wilderness that we will never forget.

My next adventure will be a long 72-mile backpack trip from west to east as I will hike the High Sierra Trail, from Giant Forest to the top of the highest mountain in the contiguous United States, Mt. Whitney.

Harrison Hawk

Sequoia Mountain Man

(a book of Adventures in the Wild – episode 13

by

Connor Corkill

High Sierra Trail

CRESCENT MEADOW

The High Sierra Trail is a long 72-mile trail from west to east on the Sierra Nevada Mountains and I really wanted to see it, even though I had already seen parts of it. Pablo wanted to go with me and I'm glad he did because he has skills that I don't have. We decided that we will catch a Greyhound Bus at Lone Pine back to Visalia after we finish the trail. We expect it to be about two weeks.

We started the hike at Crescent Meadow in the Giant Forest of the Sequoia National Park around 9 in the morning. Our first camp should be Mehrten Creek, which is about 5.5 miles from the trailhead. The trail was climbing very gradually with ups and downs that were easy to hike. After only a little over two miles we passed Panther Creek. We got to Mehrten Creek early afternoon and had to climb up a hill to the first campsite. It had a bear box. We took off our packs and checked to see if there were any more campsites. There were three more above the first one but were smaller. We rinsed off and made a small fire in the lowest camp. It wasn't the most spacious but we both squeezed our tents near the firepit side by side.

BEARPAW MEADOW

The next morning, we hiked on to Buck Canyon, where there was a larger creek. We crossed the bridge and climbed up the slope and reached Bearpaw Meadow and across from it was the famous High Sierra Camp, where many hikers stay for a few days. There was a great view of the granite peaks to the south and northeast of the camp. We camped at the lower end of the Meadow where backpackers can have a fire and more privacy. There was plenty of wood to burn for our firepit, which Pablo was happy about. There was a large tree stump about two feet high by our campsite. I filled a two-liter bottle of creek water to rinse off the sweat from my body so I took my clothes off and stood on top of the stump. As I was rinsing my body, a park ranger was walking from Little Bearpaw and saw me completely naked. She didn't say anything. She smiled and kept walking up to the ranger station. I quickly dried off and put on my clean, dry clothes.

"That's a different ranger station than the one we met earlier." Pablo said.

"Yes, she might be patrolling the area." I said.

She was a very young ranger about 20 years old. The one that we met was about 40 and heavyset. We stayed at our camp, made a nice fire and went to bed at dusk.

HAMILTON LAKE

The next morning, we got back on the trail and, as we passed by the ranger station, both rangers were sitting on the porch drinking coffee. They looked at us and the younger ranger whispered something to the other ranger's ear, pointed her finger at me and they both smiled as they waved to us. I think I know what she said.

We hiked down two miles until we got to Lone Pine Creek, where there was a bridge. We looked down and saw what looked like twisted metal and cables that were used to either carry men or supplies to an unknown destination a century ago but was destroyed by a snow storm. Continuing on through the bridge we saw the high monolith called Valhalla on the north side. We climbed another mile or so and got to Hamilton Lake. It was a beauty with excellent views of Kaweah Gap and the peaks beside it. We found a nice camp up above the lake. There were two bear boxes and one of them was full of food so there were other campers, we thought, until we saw a note on one of the duffle bags of food. It said to hold it for backpackers that needed to resupply themselves and a date when they will arrive. We used the other box and returned to our camp. Pablo and I could hear men talking but didn't see them. We looked towards the lake and saw them fishing about 100 yards away on the north side of the lake. It's amazing how far voices carry over the lake.

Eating breakfast in camp was a joy because we saved our favorite meal for that lake……Mountain House scrambled eggs and ham with potatoes and biscuits. After breakfast we packed up and started climbing the 3 miles up to Kaweah Gap.

KAWEAH GAP

As we were climbing the long and steep trail, we looked back at Hamilton Lake and took some pictures. It was a great place to camp. Just before we got to the Gap, we were walking on alpine grasses with brooks that had flowing water to refill our canteens. We passed by the mysterious-looking lake called Precipice Lake. It had ice floating on it and on the back side of it was a solid granite cliff of liquid iron, or some other material, seeping from its side which created a picturesque reflection on the lake.

While standing on the Gap, we saw the lowest lake of the Nine Lake Basin. There were no plants of any kind, only solid granite. We looked south and there was the long stretch of granite and gradually turning into pine trees called the Big Arroyo. As we walked on the Big Arroyo trail, we were seeing the Black Kaweah and the Red Kaweah mountain range in all its splendor to the east of us.

BIG ARROYO

We hiked down the 3.5 miles to a campsite beside a log cabin that was probably built by settlers many years ago. It was well-built but had claw marks from bears trying to get inside to check for food. I pointed to the trail that went west and told Pablo that it goes to Little Five Lakes, where I went on a solo trip to Black Rock Pass and those oriental guys brought a glass quart of Jack Daniels whiskey. Pablo laughed.
"I wouldn't mind having a shot of that whisky right now." he said.

We set up our camp right next to the creek. It had a nice fallen log that was perfect to sit on and it had a good size firepit. Pablo noticed there were many brook trout in the creek. He took out his nylon film vial and inside of it he had a fishing line and a small hook. He unwrapped it, caught some crickets by the creek and used them for bait, broke off a branch from a tree, connected the fishing line to it and caught ten brook trout for our dinner......ha.....amazing. Pablo is a true survivalist by figuring out how to find ways to fish in the wild.

THE GHOST

After dinner we sat by the fire and relaxed in the dark night when we heard a man's voice. We stood up and saw a very

thin man walking toward us. He had a long beard, a flannel shirt
and kaki pants. He was quiet, spoke in a low voice. He was
friendly. He said his name was John. We invited him to share
our fire's warmth. He only wanted to talk about the beauty of
the mountains and how it meant everything to him. We couldn't
see his tent or camp because of the darkness of the New Moon.
He would talk very quietly and was sincere in everything he said.
Pablo and I would just nod our heads in agreement as he talked
about nature and its beauty. We offered to give him some
Gatorade and cookies but he declined. He said he had water and
biscuits in his camp. After talking for about 20 minutes, he
thanked us and walked away into the night. Pablo and I
wondered where he was camped so after a half hour or so we
took a walk with our flashlights and looked all around but didn't
see him, his tent, or any evidence that he was even there. Later
that night, we talked about how much he looked like John Muir
and how he said he had water and biscuits in his camp.
"Was he a ghost, bro?" I asked Pablo
"I don't know but I was wondering the same thing..... spooky"
Pablo said.
We were pretty quiet for the rest of the night because it sure
felt like he wasn't real.

MORAINE LAKE

We woke up in the morning with the sun hitting our tents. We looked around to see if we could find where John was camped last night but we didn't even see any tent marks or footprints.

"Well, we've got a story to tell Nick about how we saw John Muir's ghost." I said.

We got back on the High Sierra Trail on our way to Moraine Lake. We were now on the Chagoopa Plateau, a long, flat area with the Sky Parlor Meadow on the south of it. It was a long but easy hike of about 8 miles. When we got there, the campsites were empty. We noticed the lake was very shallow near the shore and the water was warm. After choosing a campsite, we jumped into the warm water for a swim. We decided to stay an extra night in this beautiful blue lake. We had shade in our campsite with pine trees around us. On our layover day, we jumped into the lake again after breakfast but after about 30 minutes, we saw a troop of a dozen boy scouts and their leader coming up from the Big Arroyo. They passed our campsite and settled on a site far away from us. We didn't bother them and they didn't bother us. Of course, all the scouts jumped into the lake and were having fun splashing and laughing. Pablo and I were hoping they wouldn't follow us to the Kern River.

KERN RIVER

The trail down to the Kern River was steep and dangerous in some spots. It was a great view to see all the trees and vegetation surrounding the river. When we got to the bottom, I saw a Tanager, a beautiful bright yellow-colored bird that lives in the woodlands. I remember seeing them in my bird book in college. We hiked on the trail and looked back to see this high waterfall coming down from the Chagoopa Plateau. We crossed a bridge and soon came to the Kern Hot Springs. We heard someone singing Beatle songs with a guitar. He was sitting on a rock with his acoustic guitar on his lap. He sang pretty good. He looked like about our age, had long hair and was wearing a poncho.

"Hi, there…..you sound pretty good." I said.

He was surprised to see us but I could tell he was the friendly type when he welcomed us with a big smile.

"Thank you……I love the Beatles and their music." he said.

"Yes, we do too." Pablo said.

He said his name was Paul. I told him my name was Harry and Pablo was my brother.

"Where are you camped?" I asked.

"Up on the hill. It's a nice private camp." he said.

"So, you backpack with your guitar, huh? Is it heavy?" I asked.

"No, it's a three quarter size guitar…..pretty light." he answered.

He was a very nice guy and never stopped smiling, even when he talked.

"Well, my brother and I are going to find a campsite and get in the hot springs tub. Maybe we'll see you later…..sing on, my friend. You sound good." I said.

"Thanks again." he said, then started singing "Good Day Sunshine".

We found a very shady campsite about thirty yards away from the hot tub. Pablo told me to go in first, since there is only room enough for one at a time. I took some dry clothes with me and my small towel and rushed over there. I filled the tub with hot water and got in it. It was hot but I could stand it. Within a few minutes, my heart started beating faster and faster……it was beating so hard that I had to get out of the tub. I realized that I should have cooled down from the hike before getting in. My body was already too hot. We both enjoyed that hot springs tub and we were thinking about staying another night but decided to leave the next morning.

While we were eating our breakfast the next morning, we could hear the guitar man singing, "Hello Goodbye". We smiled and we started a little Indian dance around our firepit when he started singing the part "Hey la, he ba hel lo". It was great to see a musician on the trail, especially one that sings good Beatle songs.

We started walking to Junction Meadow. It was mainly flat for all seven miles. I remember being here when I met those two brothers from Lone Pine. This was a good place to have a fire in our firepit because of all the dry wood around. There was plenty of shade and the river was right next to us. There were hardly any mosquitos at the camp. That's the good thing about backpacking in September or October……not too many mosquitos. May, June, and July are the months when they really come out and bite.

CRABTREE MEADOW

The following morning, we got up at dawn, ate our breakfast of coffee, oatmeal and a protein bar. We poured water on our campfire and started to hike up Wallace Creek Trail. We climbed and climbed until we hit the John Muir Trail. When we got there, we turned south, passed Sandy Meadow and got to Crabtree Meadow by mid-afternoon. We were running low on food and we saw three bear boxes. Sometimes hikers leave their food in them for other hikers when they have extra, want to surprise other backpackers, or don't want to carry the extra weight up to Mt. Whitney, since they will be out and over the mountain in one more leg. I opened one box and 'lo and behold', there was a large zip-lock plastic bag with the best tasting beef jerky either of us had ever tried. Whoever made it had the perfect recipe with those spices in them. We were lucky to find that tasty jerky. We sat on the grass and finished eating the jerky and wondered where to set up our camp.

THE COWBOY

After a short time later, we saw a horse packer riding his horse and leading four mules. He came up to us and I waved, hoping we could talk to him.

"HI, there, partner. Do you know where the campsites are?" I asked

"I'm going to one right now that's pretty big. I don't mind sharing it." he said.

We followed him and his equestrian team to a large area surrounded by cottonwood trees and a grassy meadow next to it. He dismounted his horse, took off his saddle and placed it on a log. He then took the pack saddles off of the mules and let them graze in the grass of the meadow. He was dressed like a cowboy with all the right clothing, including hat, boots, belt buckle, and even boot spurs.

"There'll be some backpackers comin' soon." he said

"I just dropped off some food and other supplies at the Crabtree Ranger Station for 'em." the cowboy said.

"They'll be comin' up later on, hikin' up from Rock Creek with day packs, I reckon." he continued.

"Where are you stationed?" I asked.

"Cottonwood Horse Stables. I'll leave back tomorrow morning." he said.

He then took four medium-sized logs and threw them in the firepit. He grabbed a gas can from a pack saddle and poured gas right on the logs. He struck a wooden match on his belt buckle and threw it in the firepit. It was like a scene in a western movie of the 1850's. This guy looked, talked, and acted like a real cowboy. The flame was three feet high before it settled down to two as he added some kindling. He put his saddle blanket on the ground and, with his saddle as a pillow, laid on the blanket, covered his body with a wool blanket and tipped his cowboy hat over his eyes, gave us a little wave with his hand and said, "'night, boys". Pablo and I looked at each other and smiled. It's like we were in a time machine back in the 1800's watching a cowboy on the trail.

The next morning, we woke up and the cowboy was gone. He must have been really quiet or we were just too tired to hear anything. We ate a bigger breakfast than usual because we were going to try to see Mt. Whitney then go all the way to Whitney Portal in one day, if possible. As we were packing up our bags, we noticed a black trash bag that wasn't mine nor Pablo's. We looked inside and there were about ten protein bars. The cowboy left it for us. He was a good dude. We split the ten between us and started our hike up to Mt. Whitney.

When we got to Guitar Lake, we saw many orange-colored frogs on the edge of the lake. They were brightly colored and very small.

"Bro, I know about these frogs. They are endangered. Let's just take pictures and go on our way." I said.

"The lake is shaped like a guitar and the frogs are gathered on the head and neck of the guitar. We'll be able to see the shape better when we climb up the mountain." Pablo said.

MT. WHITNEY

The trail was rough because some of the granite rocks had sharp edges so we had to be careful not to step on them. We saw Mt. Hitchcock on the south side. We circled around a switchback and at 13, 480 feet in elevation, we looked back and could see Guitar Lake shaped exactly like a guitar. We also saw some spots that looked like some backpackers had moved granite rocks around so they could lay their sleeping bags to sleep overnight. They also made windbreakers with larger granite rocks. When we got to Trail Crest, we took our packs off, leaned them against rocks and hiked to see the hut in the summit of Mt. Whitney. When we got there, a group of hikers were already there looking over the view and taking pictures. Pablo and I signed the register and took some pictures too. "Nick will want to see these pics of the summit." Pablo said. "Yes, he wants some proof that we actually made it up here." I said as we laughed.

We hiked down the 99 switchbacks to Trail Camp. We took a break and wondered if we should camp there with other campers or take a chance and go down the mountain on the east side. We ate two protein bars each, that the cowboy gave us, and decided to go down to Whitney Portal. When we got down the mountain, we were about to fall from exhaustion but we dragged our legs and made it. We got a ride with an old man that had a pickup truck and he took us to the Greyhound Bus depot where we bought our tickets and got in the bus to Visalia, California.

It was a very adventurous backpack trip that we will never forget. Since it was already September, it was too late to begin another high elevation backpack trip that year.
"Next year I am going to backpack the John Muir Trail, bro." I said.
"I'll try to go with you but I'm not sure I will, since I'll be going to Alaska with a friend and do some salmon fishing." Pablo said.
"Well, whatever happens, happens, brother." I said.
We leaned back on our seats and ate another cowboy protein bar.

"These protein bars are really good, bro. The cowboy helped us to finish the trip." I said.

"Yes, he did." Pablo said.

We munched on them, leaned back on our seats and slowly fell asleep.

as we passed the bow hunters camp, we noticed that only one was keeping watch while the rest of the hunters were still asleep in their tents. We hiked over Farewell Gap and down to Mineral King Valley.

We had another adventurous backpack trip that started in Sequoia National Park, moved to The Golden Trout Wilderness, back to the Park, then again to the GTW, and finally back to the National Park. We will call Nick to pick us up tomorrow, since it will be Saturday. Pablo and I have had some momentous times in the wilderness that we will never forget.

My next adventure will be a long 72-mile backpack trip from west to east as I will hike the High Sierra Trail, from Giant Forest to the top of the highest mountain in the contiguous United States, Mt. Whitney.

Harrison Hawk

Sequoia Mountain Man

(a book of Adventures in the Wild – episode 14)

by

Connor Corkill

The John Muir Trail

YOSEMITE VALLEY

The most popular trail on the west side of the Sierra Nevada Mountains is the John Muir Trail. It is a 211-mile trail extending from Yosemite Valley to the top of Mt. Whitney. The breathtaking granite monoliths of El Capitan and Half Dome are known throughout the world where millions of visitors come every year to see the splendor and awe of the Yosemite Valley.

My friend, Nick, dropped me off here and said he will pick me up at Whitney Portal at the end of my trip. Pablo could not go with me this time but will join Nick in Whitney Portal. I started at the trailhead in Happy Isles Nature Center, at 4,033 feet elevation. I mailed a box of food and supplies to myself in care of Vermillion Resort at Edison Lake, which is about the halfway point to Mt. Whitney. I climbed a little over 2,000 feet to Little Yosemite Valley where I camped for the first night. There were many campsites and I was lucky enough to find a good one before they were all taken. In the morning, I continued the climb and passed the Half Dome junction and Cloud's Rest. I had two maps for this trip, the Tom Harrison map, because it shows mileage from one leg to another, and Trails Illustrated map, because it has a better visual of topography. I reached Cathedral Pass at 9,700 feet and at the base of it was Cathedral Lake. I was tempted to camp there, especially with a great view of Cathedral Peak, but I wanted to reach Tuolumne Meadows and camp there.

TUOLUMNE MEADOWS

Tuolumne Meadows is a true wonderland with a vast open area of Ponderosa trees, round smooth-shaped granite boulders, and grass spread over the meadow all the way to the base of Mt. Lyell. The ranger station is right next to the JMT. I bought a few picture postcards of Yosemite and mailed them to my friends and to my Mom and Dad in London, England. I walked to the area that is reserved for backpackers. We are allowed to camp there overnight free of charge but for only one night. There were many backpackers there and I met some very nice folks. I pitched my tent and cooked my dinner on my propane stove. I was warned that we will most likely get a visit from a bear or two during the night, since some campers don't follow the rules about food storage. The bear boxes were packed with duffle bags full of food but I squeezed mine in.

The next morning, I started my hike alongside the Tuolumne River, which is very flat for about 7 miles. When I got to Lyell Base Camp, I found a flat area to pitch my tent and it was a good campsite to rest and build up my energy before climbing Donahue Pass. I was starting to regret carrying 70 lbs. on my back because it was starting to feel like 100 lbs., but it was mainly 30 lbs. of food that I thought I would need until I would get to Vermillion Resort and pick up my box of supplies.

I climbed over Donahue Pass the next morning. It was a little over 11,000 feet and my backpack was really taking a toll on my back. I was seriously thinking about getting rid of some of my food to ease the pain but I wanted to climb over Island Pass at 10,200 feet and maybe camp and rest my bones for two nights.

At mile 43, I went over the Pass and found a place to camp at Thousand Islands Lake. It was a huge lake with many small islands on it. As I was resting at the camp, I saw a man with a strange backpack walking towards the lake. When he got to the edge of the lake, he took off his pack, unfolded it twice and then I realized that it was a one-man kayak. He got in it and started paddling towards one of the small islands. I sat down by the trail and from sheer exhaustion, I fell asleep. I woke up in the middle of the night with a fever and caught a cold. I realized that I didn't even open my sleeping bag so I pulled it out and got in it. My head was hurting so bad and as I touched by forehead, it was a high fever. With the pain and body heat making it hard to move, I passed out.

KYRA

When I woke up, I saw a beautiful woman's face looking at me. She had one hand supporting my head and was giving me water from a canteen.

"Are you an angel?" I asked.

She smiled and gave me more water.

"No, I'm not an angel. My name is Kyra.....here, drink more water. How do you feel?" she asked.

"I dreamed that I died and went to heaven." I answered.

"No, you're not dead but you have a very high fever." she said.

"How long have I been passed out?" I said.

"I don't really know but I've been with you since yesterday morning." she said.

"I was afraid you were dead when I passed by you on my way south. What's your name?" she continued.

"Harrison Hawk." I said.

"Harrison, I'm a nurse so I had to see if I could help you. I'm backpacking to Mt. Whitney but when I touched your forehead, I knew you had a fever so I stayed." she said.

Kyra stayed with me for two more days, feeding me and keeping me warm inside my sleeping bag. I eventually got better, thanks to her.

"Where are you backpacking to?" she asked.

"I'm going to Mt. Whitney." I said.

"Maybe we can go together. I'll hike with you for a couple of days in case you need help along the way." she said.

I feel like she saved my life and I told her so. She said that any nurse would have done the same thing. No, I thought, she just has a big heart and compassion for people in need.

We passed Garnet Lake and marveled at the great Minarets mountain range, one of the most beautiful mountain ranges on the JMT. The Minarets peaks resemble The Alps of Europe. We went over Gladys Pass and made a camp at Trinity Lakes. I was still weak from the fever that had taken over my body. Kyra kept watching over me, checking my temperature with her thermometer every once in a while.

DEVIL'S POSTPILE

We hiked into Devil's Postpile, a wall of hexagonal columns almost 60 feet high. The Devil's Postpile is also a National Monument. People can drive their vehicles to it, since Mammoth Lakes had roads to the highest lakes of the Sierra Nevada mountains. We also couldn't wait to have a hot meal in a restaurant at Red's Meadow. After buying a few supplies from the grocery store, we went to the restaurant and I bought Kyra a dinner of her choosing. We both had hot meals and it was a great change from what we were eating on the trail. There was also a building with some private rooms that had a tub is each one connected to the hot springs. There was no electricity in the rooms so we had to take our own battery powered lanterns or candles. I told Kyra to go to the only stall that was open. She took her dry clothes and a towel. She forgot to take a candle so I walked in to give it to her and saw her completely naked standing in the tub. Her body was absolutely beautiful and with her long black hair, she looked like a model for one of Michelangelo's body sculptures. She quickly turned around when I surprised her. I apologized for walking in unannounced but gave her the candle. I couldn't get over her amazing 5'8" stature. I took my turn in the tub after she was finished. We camped overnight at the campground next door and it was so great to be completely clean in that hot springs water for a change.

We hiked 8 miles the next day and found a nice campsite at Duck's Lake. We should have hiked farther, since I lost at least 2 days with the fever but I guess I was still feeling the effects from it. At mile #74, we came to Tully's Hole but as soon as we got there, there was a swarm of mosquitoes attacking us. There must have been millions of them. We put on our mosquito head nets and rushed out of there as fast as we could.

SILVER PASS LAKE

After going over Silver Pass, we stayed at the same campsite that Pablo and I stayed the previous year. I told Kyra what happened to Pablo and what we had to go through to get out of there.
"I now know what kind of man you are, Harrison, by taking all those steps to save your brother." Kyra said.

"Well, sometimes we have to switch our minds into 'survival mode' to get out alive." I said.

I told her about the lion and that I hoped it won't come while we're there. She suggested that we should not cook any aromatic foods so the lion won't smell it. We ate dry food that night and she held my hand as we watched the stars on that clear and quiet night.

The next morning, we hiked down to Cliff Meadow, as Pablo and I called it. I told Kyra that it was the place where we camped twice and saw the horse group that wanted to help us at Silver Pass Lake. We didn't camp there and wanted to hike all the way to Edison Lake and pick up my box of supplies at Vermillion Resort. We got to the boarding dock and waited for the ferry to pick us up.

EDISON LAKE

We saw the ferry coming in the afternoon and we boarded. The driver recognized me from last years trip. He was bringing two backpackers with him. I introduced him to Kyra and we couldn't wait to get to the resort and claim a spot in the backpacker's tent. When we got to the resort, we headed straight to the tent and no one was there. We chose two cots and laid our packs there. I went to pick up my box of supplies and brought it back to the tent. I now had more food, fuel, toilet paper, etc. and filled my pack full again. Kyra still had food in her pack but it was mainly protein bars and other freeze-dried foods. We went to the restaurant and ordered dinner plates before we turned in for the night. That evening we laid out our sleeping bags on our cots and got ready to sleep for the night but before she laid on her cot, she came and kissed me on the lips. We embraced and just before anything else could happen, three backpackers walked into the tent for their free night. Kyra and I looked at each other and smiled as we shrugged our shoulders. I had a good feeling that Kyra and I would be good friends after our trip was over. She asked me if she could hike with me all the way to Mt. Whitney. I told her that I was hoping she would.

The next leg of our hike was a long one....13 miles and I'm glad we filled our canteens full of water because it was hard to find a creek during that leg. We camped at Marie Lake, which was near the base of Seldon Pass. It was a pretty easy climb at only 10,860 feet. We continued on to Sally Keys Lakes where we saw two men fishing. We could see the fish jumping all over the lake. It was a fisherman's paradise. We made friends with the fishermen and they gave us four fish, since they were catching them almost as soon as they threw in their hooks in the water. They were from San Francisco on vacation. We told them that we had just camped at Marie Lakes, which was only two or three miles away so they wrapped the fish in foil paper and told us to cook them when we get to our next camp. They were really nice guys. We thanked them and we went on our way.

We hiked another long leg and made it to Evolution Meadow and soon to McClure Meadow, where we camped after a long 17-mile hike. We cooked the four trout on my camp stove and added some couscous as a side dish. It was fantastic. There was a ranger station but he or she was on patrol. There was a sign on the door that said so. We saw a big buck walking on the shallow creek and we took pictures and agreed that this area was one of the most peaceful spots on the trail.

At mile #128, we took a break at Sapphire Lake, refilled out canteens then started the climb to Muir Pass.

THUNDER AND LIGHTNIING

It was a hard climb to the top of Muir Pass. There was a stone hut built there by the Sierra Club many years ago and it was a good thing that it was there as dark clouds started forming above us. Before long, it started to rain and we heard rolling thunder so we quickly got inside the hut. We then heard the loud claps of thunder. We looked outside the doorway and saw lightning flashing across the sky. We stayed dry and warm in the hut and huddled together and after 20 minutes or so, a man and a woman rushed into the hut drenched with water from the rainstorm. They were from England and it showed because of their strong accent, as we Americans call it. I told them that my mother was from London and that her side of the family would breed racehorses. The woman was also a nurse and she and Kyra started having a long conversation while the man and I talked about the storm and hoped it would stop soon. The storm eventually passed over us after an hour so we went on our way down. We said our goodbyes and wished each other luck. We started seeing snow patches here and there on the way down to

Helen Lake, where we camped after a long 11-mile hike. When we got there, I pitched my tent and told Kyra that she didn't have to pitch hers. We could stay in mine and we'd be warmer in our sleeping bags in one tent. She agreed and got into my tent. We were pretty exhausted and we went straight to sleep for the night.

The next morning, we had coffee and breakfast from my food bag. Helen Lake was huge. The day was clear and sunny so we wanted to make it to Grouse Meadow for our next camp, which was 10 miles away. On the way there, we went by Le Conte Canyon, where there is supposed to be a ranger station but it wasn't visible from the trail. As we continued on the trail, we saw an old man hiking down from the Dusy Basin junction. He was leading a donkey, which was carrying his pack. We waved at him and he waved back with a big smile. We continued on and soon there was another surprise. It was a man sitting on a folding chair watching over three Llamas. The rest of his group was probably taking a day hike somewhere but it was a nice surprise to see Llamas on the JMT. They have hoofs that are easy on the trail, compared to horses with their larger and more trail-damaging hoofs.

At mile #138, we got to Grouse Meadow and found a good campsite. I told Kyra that Nick was picking me up at Whitney Portal and I was hoping I wouldn't be late. She told me that her sister was picking her up and she had a walkie-talkie that picks up a satellite signal and hopefully she can tell her to wait for her in case we are late. We got up early the next morning and hiked to Palisades Lake, which was near the base of Mather Pass. It was the next pass we will have to go over.

SNOW-COVERED TRAIL

When we got to the base of Mather Pass, we realized it was on the north side of the mountain and the trail was covered with snow. The sun doesn't hit the north side as much as it does on the south side so we should always expect more snow on the north side. We weren't sure where the trail was but we could see the Pass high above us. Neither one of us were carrying crampons so we might have a hard time walking on the snow that was steep most of the way. We started our climb slowly on the snowy, perilous trail. When we were about 100 yards into our climb, Kyra stepped on snow that gave way. She slipped and slid down the snow trail about 30 yards, hitting her head on a boulder and she started bleeding from her forehead. I rushed down to help her and noticed she was dizzy and incoherent. I took off my pack and pulled out my first aid kit. I pressed on her forehead to stop the bleeding, then wrapped a bandage around her head. I tried to think about what to do but I was in a panic. I moved her body to a side boulder that was clear of snow and told her that I will take my pack up to the Pass, drop it off and come back, carry her pack and help her go up. I looked at the large boulders to the side of the snow trail. I decided to climb up to the Pass by maneuvering from one boulder to another until I'd reach the top. I thought I would get up to the Pass faster than walking in the snow. I had my heavy pack on but managed to do it. When I got to the Pass, I took off my pack and leaned it against another large boulder and started to slowly slide down the snow trail, breaking my fall with my boots until I reached her. I put her pack on my back and helped her up. Slowly, we started the climb on the snow. I made sure that I had a good grip around her waist as we hiked up. I looked at her forehead and she was starting to bleed again. The blood was dripping over her right eye so I stopped and, in my panic, realized that I left my first aid kit in my pack, which was at the Pass. I fumbled through her pack to find her first aid kit. When I found it, I took out some gauze and re-wrapped her head. She was still oozy from the hit on her head. We continued on and after an hour, that seemed like three hours, we reached the Pass. We rested for awhile until she came to her senses. We were now at 12,100 feet elevation and one mile away we could see Lake Marjorie. I took off her pack and put it on her back. I put my pack on my back and we started the descent. We walked down the mountain and as we got to the lake, I laid her down softly and we rested. Her bleeding stopped. I pitched my tent and laid out our sleeping bags inside. I helped her to get inside her sleeping bag and I walked to the lake to fill our canteens. We stayed at the lake for two nights until she felt strong enough to start hiking again. We knew that our next leg was to go over Pinchot Pass, which was also 12,100 feet. She was feeling stronger now. "Harrison, you did it again.....first you helped Pablo and now you helped me." she said.

"You should join the 'search and rescue' team. They would make you 'captain'." she said smiling.

"Survival mode." I said, and I kissed her.

RAE LAKES

We hiked over Pinchot Pass with no problem and soon came to Rae Lakes. We could see Fin Dome as we got closer to Arrowhead Lake. We wanted to camp at the lake closest to the ranger station, in case Kyra got worse from the fall. I called out to the ranger and she came out of her station. I told her what happened and she re-bandaged Kyra's forehead and gave her pain pills in case she gets worse. We camped there for one night then left the next morning. The climb to Glen Pass was a long one. We passed the junction to Charlotte Lake and found a nice camp near Center Basin. We rested up for our next and highest Pass on the JMT....Forester Pass at 13,150.

When we were about ¾ of the way up the mountain, we came to a plateau and saw a large group of backpackers with tents already set. I talked to one of them and he said they were Sierra Club members and the group was planning on going north to Rae Lakes. Kyra and I hiked on over Forrester Pass and went down to Tyndall Creek camp. I had been there before on my Colby Lake trip. It was very cold there, especially when the wind blows. Kyra tried to contact her sister on the walkie-talkie but couldn't get a good signal, possibly because of a weak battery. We thought that she may have turned it on accidently when she fell on the snow and depleted the battery energy. We heated water for our ramen noodles and freeze-dried beans. We talked about Nick and Kyra's sister, Jane, and hoped that they would wait for us if we were late.

The next day, we left and, after crossing Tyndall Creek, saw a pond with orange-colored frogs. I told Kyra that they were the same species that I saw at Guitar Lake the year before and that they were endangered. We climbed up to Bighorn Plateau, a huge, flat area with giant boulders that were spread out as if they were dropped there by volcanic forces millions of years ago (or by space aliens). It was eerie. Hiking on, we finally came to Crabtree Meadow, the last meadow that we will see on the John Muir Trail. I told her about the jerky that we found in a bear box and the cowboy from Cottonwood Stables that Pablo and I camped with last year. She enjoyed hearing the stories that I experienced the last few years in the wilderness, which were great backpacking adventures. We found a nice camp and stayed only one night because we were both two days late on our meetups with Nick and Jane. The next day, we passed Guitar Lake and saw the orange-colored frogs. We re-filled out canteens and started the climb to Mt. Whitney.

MT. WHITNEY

Kyra and I hiked slowly up the mountain, looking back from time to time to enjoy the view. We saw Mt. Hitchcock and Guitar Lake and soon got to Trail Crest, where we took off our packs and went on to the summit. When we got to the stone shelter, we took pictures and signed the register. Some rain clouds started forming over the mountain so we quickly went back to our packs and went down the 99 switchbacks to Trail Camp. When we got there, I was surprised to see my brother, Pablo, waiting for us.

"Hey, brother, you finally made it." Pablo said.

We embraced in a big hug. I introduced him to Kyra and we sat down and I explained what happened and why we were late by two days.

"Nick is down at Whitney Portal. He rented a motorhome but I wanted to climb up here and meet you, in case you were in trouble." Pablo said.

Kyra wanted to hurry and get down because her sister would be waiting for her in a car. We hurried on down the mountain after resting for an hour. When we got to Whitney Portal, Pablo pointed to the motorhome and we walked toward it. Kyra went to look for her sister and said she will come back to the motorhome after she finds her. Nick came out of the motorhome. We embraced and he said he had a surprise for me. The side door of the motorhome opened and my mother and father walked out.

"Hello, son." my mother said as she gave me a big hug and a kiss on the cheek.

"Mom, Dad, what a great surprise." I said.

My Dad gave me a big hug and we went back inside the motorhome.

"Son, we got your postcard that you sent us and decided to come and surprise you for your great achievement." Mom said.

"We are both very proud of you, son." my Dad said.

After talking for a few minutes, I remembered about Kyra.

"Mom, Dad, Pablo, Nick, this woman named Kyra saved my life and I want you to meet her." I said.

I walked out the motorhome and as I did, Kyra and her sister were walking towards me. Kyra introduced me to Jane and I invited them into the motorhome.

I introduced Kyra and Jane to my parents and Nick. Kyra and I sat next to each other, held hands and everyone got excited waiting for us to speak.

"Boy, have I got some stories to tell you" I said.

I started to tell them about my first solo backpacking trip at Southfork Campground, Hockett Meadow and all the other backpacking adventures that I experienced, one by one. I told them that I wanted to see, hear, and feel what my ancestors did. They were excited and happy to hear what happened to me.....the joys, the tears, the dangers and how I managed to get through them with Pablo or by myself.

I will cherish them in my memory for the rest of my life.

THE END